FISH
IN THE
SKY

FISH
IN THE
SKY

Fridrik Erlings

CANDLEWICK PRESS

Copyright © 2008 by Fridrik Erlings
Published by arrangement with Meadowside Children's Books,
185 Fleet Street, London EC4A 2HS

Hymn on page 65 by Valdimar Briem; translated by Bernard Scudder

Hymn on page 69 by Steingrím Thorsteinsson; translated by Bernard Scudder

Verse from "Hear the joyful news from throne up high,"
by Rev. Magnús Guðmundsson used by permission from YMCA/YWCA
Reykjavík, Iceland. Translated by Bernard Scudder

First U.S. edition 2012

Library of Congress Cataloging-in-Publication Data
Fridrik Erlingsson, date.
Fish in the sky / Fridrik Erlings. —1st U.S. ed.
p. cm.
Summary: Josh Stephenson's thirteenth year starts with a baffling sequence of events, including an odd gift from his estranged father, the arrival of his flirty seventeen-year-old female cousin, locker-room teasing about certain embarrassing anatomical changes, and wondering if dreams of love can ever come true.
ISBN 978-0-7636-5888-5
[1. Coming of age—Fiction. 2. High schools—Fiction. 3. Schools—Fiction. 4. Single-parent families—Fiction. 5. Cousins—Fiction. 6. Dating (Social customs)—Fiction.] I. Title.
PZ7.F89586Fis 2012
[Fic]—dc23   2011048348

12 13 14 15 16 17 BVG 10 9 8 7 6 5 4 3 2 1

Printed in Berryville, VA, U.S.A.

This book was typeset in Adobe Caslon.

Candlewick Press
99 Dover Street
Somerville, Massachusetts 02144

visit us at www.candlewick.com

To the memory of
Bernard Scudder

Chapter 1

I am a star, a twinkling star. I'm an infant on the edge of a grave and an old man in a cradle, both a fish in the sky and a bird in the sea. I'm a boy on the outside but a girl on the inside, innocent in body, guilty in soul.

Light seeps through my eyelids. I blink twice and glance at the alarm clock. It's exactly thirteen years and twenty-four minutes since the moment I was born into this world, on that cold February morning, when a Beatles song played for Mom on the radio. She went into labor and the midwife came running into the room, arriving almost too late because she'd gotten stuck in a snowdrift on the way, and screamed, "You're not seriously thinking of giving birth in this weather, are you?"

Mom and Dad had danced to the Beatles' "Love Me Do" nine months earlier at some dance somewhere, and it had since become their song. Then it became my song.

I'm a year closer to being considered a grown-up, as Mom likes to put it, with a shadow of apprehension in her voice. But until then I'm just as far from being considered a grown-up as I am from being a child; I'm the missing link in the evolution of *Homo sapiens*.

I sit up in my blue-striped pajamas and look around. My desk is still in its place under the window, the bookshelves by the wall, the fish tank on the chest of drawers in the corner. Everything is as it should be. Nothing has changed, and yet it's as if everything has changed.

Then I notice a cardboard box in the middle of the floor that wasn't there when I went to bed. It's about thirty inches high and fifteen wide, tied with string and brown tape, battered looking, with dented corners and oil stains, as if it has been stored in a ship's engine room for a long time. Which it obviously has. This could only be a gift from Dad that someone snuck into my room after I fell asleep. Dad's packages don't always arrive on the right day. Sometimes they don't arrive at all. But he always sends me a postcard, wherever he goes. Dad works on a big freighter and sails all over the world. I get cards from Rio, Hamburg, Bremen, Cuxhaven, and places like that, and I put them all up on the wall over my bed. I know it's not always easy for a sailor to get to a post office on time to send a card or a package. I could easily understand that. But what is more difficult to figure out is why Dad seems to be so much farther away from me when he's ashore. But then when I think about that, I turn into a girl inside and get tears in my eyes at the thought that Dad's gift has arrived at all, and what's more, on the right day.

It'll soon be a year since I last saw him. He showed up with my birthday present three weeks late and was drunk and demanded coffee. Mom scolded him like a dog for turning up in such a state and setting such a terrible example, now that he was finally making an appearance, and asked him if there was a rule against phoning from those ships, and whether he couldn't at least have tried to call me on my birthday. He apologized profusely and said they couldn't, it wasn't his fault, they were at sea. Then he bent over and kissed me on both cheeks, and the stench of him was so strong I could still smell it in my hair after he had gone—a powerful mixture of Old Spice and beer, of course.

Then Mom closed the door, and he stood there in front of it, muttering something, and then staggered into the taxi that was waiting for him. That was almost a year ago.

I take my penknife out of the desk drawer and turn to face the box. It doesn't smell only of oil but also as if it was kept in a cold hold under stacks of oranges and soap. I stick the blade of the knife into one corner and calmly slice through the cardboard.

Two coal-black eyes stare at me from the depths of the box through a mass of hay and crumpled newspaper. A sharp, curved beak looks as if it's snatching at me. I jump to my feet, and my heart skips a beat and my knees wobble like they're about to fall off. I take cover behind the desk, bend a little, and try to figure out what it is. I can make out two wings from behind the straw, poised for flight.

It's a stuffed falcon with a gaping beak, beady black eyes, and sharp claws firmly clutching a piece of red volcanic rock. I kneel on the floor and cautiously stretch my sweaty hands into the straw, drag the falcon out, and place him up on the desk.

The falcon stares at me with his fiery eyes as I drop into my desk chair. This is the greatest birthday present anyone has ever given me.

And what's more, this isn't just any falcon, no ordinary stuffed falcon that anyone could pick up at an antique shop, covered in dust and muck. No, this is a famous falcon who's been on TV and whose picture has appeared in the press and who's squawked in interviews on the lunchtime news on the radio; this is Christian the Ninth in person. Well, what's left of him.

He tumbled onto the *Orca*, the ship Dad works on, sometime last year and was named after a cook called Christian the Ninth because he was the ninth cook who had worked on the ship. The bird was exhausted and more dead than alive, but Dad nursed him back to life and fed him. And the falcon became so fond of him that no one else but Dad was allowed to go near him. When the ship pulled into harbor, the local press was waiting for them and the falcon sat on my father's shoulder like a parrot on some fierce pirate and ate raw meat. When the time came to release him again, the bird refused to leave and flew back onto the ship and sat on the bridge. When the ship sailed back out to sea, the falcon was still on board. And when Dad came up on deck, the bird flew off the bridge and perched on his shoulder. They were inseparable. But on one trip, the bird got sick and refused to eat. By the time the ship came back to land, the falcon was in the care of his namesake, the cook, inside an icebox. And now Dad has had him stuffed to give to me as a birthday present.

Thinking about it, I realize that it could only have been Dad who'd snuck into my room with the box. Does that mean that he's staying with Auntie Carol as he normally does when he's ashore? Or has he maybe gone to the country, where Suzy, his new girlfriend, lives?

There is a piece of string tied around one of the falcon's legs with a small note attached. On it is a message written with an almost inkless ballpoint pen: *To Mister Josh Stephenson. A very happy birthday. Your dad.*

If I were just a tiny bit older, I'm sure I wouldn't have these tears in my eyes. It's the words *your dad* that bring out the girl in me and make me weak all over again. Even though I'm thirteen years old and shouldn't be like this, I'm still not old enough to be able to pretend I don't feel anything.

The door opens behind me, and Mom is standing there with open arms, in her pajamas and bathrobe, holding a package that I immediately guess is a book.

"You're not seriously thinking of giving birth in this weather, are you?" she shouts, pulling me into an embrace. Then she looks at me with a scrutinizing air, as if I were a newborn in her arms and she were trying to find some family trait, some proof that I'm definitely hers and no one else's.

"Is it really thirteen years? Imagine, thirteen years." She sighs, all misty eyed.

It's a constant source of puzzlement to her, how the years have flown since the day of my birth. Every birthday she repeats the words of that midwife who almost came too late to deliver me, as if it all happened only yesterday. Time seems to stand still during the other days of the year for her. Neither Christmas nor New Year's seems to trigger this awareness of the passing of time, not even her own birthday. It's as if the day of my birth was the only milestone in her life that really meant anything to her.

"Happy birthday, Josh, sweetie, and this is for you," she says, holding out the package to me, stroking my hair with her palm and then my cheek with her knuckle.

I tear the wrapping away and a huge black book with a gilded cross on the cover appears. It's a Bible. The pages are thin and rustly, and the lettering is as tiny as a flyspeck. Mom warned me that she was going to give me the Bible because the time had come for me to start reading God's word, the story of creation and the New Testament, and to stop reading comics and those trivial juvenile books that are all about criminals and spies and are all trash. Books like that could only give you twisted ideas about life; in worst-case scenarios, they could even turn you into a criminal. And this was why I dropped out of Sunday school and didn't want to go to the YMCA's summer camp last year and learn how to sail a boat and play soccer and sing about Jesus like all the other good boys. Now I could have a good read of the

Bible and learn everything that needed to be known about Genesis and Jesus Christ before my confirmation next year.

"God Almighty," she says, staring at the erect falcon scowling at her from the desk. "A stuffed bird! Is he out of his mind?"

"Did he come yesterday?" I ask.

"He's gone bananas."

"Mom," I say.

"Yes, he came," she says. "At about midnight and wanted to talk to you because he was on his way to the country. It took some work to get rid of him. A stuffed bird! What next?"

"I would have wanted to see him," I say, trying to fight back that shameful girlishness that's quivering inside me.

"Yes, well, he's not coming into my house drunk, that's for sure, and he knows that perfectly well. He'll call from the country, honey, if he can get a signal," she adds, sitting beside me on the bed. I know what she's going to say now. She's going to tell me the story about my ear infection and its miraculous healing through the Bible.

"I didn't own a Bible until I was twenty," she says. "But I didn't read it until long after that," she adds, stroking my head. "That was when I had to stay up watching over you when you had that ear infection. Then I prayed that you would be OK, because you cried so hard and there was nothing I could do for you but read the Bible out loud. And then you fell asleep just like that, and the next day you were fine again. It was a miracle."

Although I am eternally grateful to have been delivered from my ear infection through a miracle from the Bible that occurred in a remote past I can no longer remember, I can't stop thinking that Dad came and wanted to see me.

"Yes, it was definitely a miracle," she says distractedly, standing up to gather the straw and rolled-up newspapers on the floor. She squeezes them back into the box, muttering something about what an utterly ludicrous idea it was of his to give me a stuffed bird.

Could it be that back then I fell asleep out of sheer boredom? But of course I don't say that out loud. That's no way to talk about the Bible.

The majestic work of creation stands before me on my desk, frozen for eternity like a photograph: outstretched wings, swollen chest, menacing beak, claws clinging to the rock. The falcon, *Falco rusticolus*, is a wondrous sight to behold when he glides through the sky and dives at two hundred miles an hour to catch his prey and snatch it in his claws like a thunderbolt. The ptarmigan is his favorite victim. He himself has no enemies to fear and rules over the heavens like a king.

According to legend, the Virgin Mary once convened all the birds of the world and ordered them to walk through fire to prove their faith and devotion to her. In those days, falcons and ptarmigans were like brother and sister and loved and admired each other. But the ptarmigan was cowardly and didn't dare to cross the fire. That is why its legs are still furry, and the legs of other birds are singed to the skin. The Virgin Mary was angry with the ptarmigan and decreed that she would be the most vulnerable and defenseless of all birds, and the bird that everyone would want to hunt, particularly her brother, the falcon. This is why the falcon prefers to hunt the ptarmigan and singles her out to kill and eat. But once he has ripped her breast open and seen her heart, he recognizes his sister again. That triggers off a torrent of sorrow in him and pitiful weeping that echoes between the rocks and cliffs for a very long time afterward. But he can't control his nature; despite the grief it causes him, he has to hunt his beloved sister.

I wonder if Dad feels like that when he thinks of Mom. Does Mom still long for him? If I hadn't been born, Mom might have married some farmer up north, and Dad someone else too in the end. I only exist because they happened to meet at that country ball and danced together to that Beatles song. Maybe I was never supposed to exist. Maybe that was a miracle too.

My book lies on the desk: *Life and Creation* by Josh Stephenson, a thick exercise book I use to record anything of importance in life. I've come to realize that by observing nature and the animal kingdom with a scientific eye, you can actually learn to understand the things that really matter in life and creation. I open the book and start to draw the falcon at the top of the page. First the outline with a dark pencil and then the shadows with a softer one, drawing in the detail of his fine feathers, the pride in his chest, the fierceness of his piercing gaze, the power in the sharp claws clutching the rock. Then, below, I write down absolutely everything I know about the falcon, starting off with the story of why he started to hunt the ptarmigan. It's only a folktale, of course, but it somehow seems to contain a lot more truth than many of the other stories that are supposed to be authentic and real. And why doesn't the ptarmigan protect herself? Isn't it because deep down she wants to be caught by the falcon? Doesn't she long for his embrace even though she knows it will be her last? They're lovers that can only ever meet at the moment of her death; for a brief moment, they can look each other in the eye and see themselves in their true light. Then it's all over.

And the falcon flies high up into the heavens and weeps.

Chapter 2

Peter Johnson, my friend and classmate, is on the doorstep. He puffs up his chest and gives me a stiff salute, clicking his heels and striking a stern military pose, puffy cheeked, auburn haired, short fingered.

"Reporting for duty, Sergeant Stephenson!"

This is how we've been greeting each other ever since we saw some comedy about the army at Peter's house, sometime when we were eleven.

And I do the same—give him a stiff salute, puff out my chest, and strike the same macho military pose that Peter finds so funny—and say, "At ease, Private Johnson."

Then his face cracks into a smile and he laughs because he still thinks it's a really funny routine. And that's the only way we ever greet each other.

"Happy birthday!" he says, handing me a package.

Sometimes Peter and I are like brothers, because we share the same interests—natural history and zoology—but other times we're about as alike as chalk and cheese. Unlike me, there's nothing that can knock him off-balance; he's always the same, never too sulky but never too happy either, more kind of even keeled. Maybe it's good he's that way, because he's got five sisters—two older, three younger— and there's hardly a moment's peace in his house.

Mom ushers Peter into the living room, where my dad's sister, Auntie Carol, is sitting. Mom always invites her to my birthdays. That's because Carol is such a good person, as Mom likes to put it. And because she makes the best pear tart in the world, and for as long as I can remember, she's always turned up to my birthday parties with a pear tart. But only then, never on other occasions. For the other 364 days of the year, I can only dream of such a treat. Auntie Carol's pear tarts are so good that there's just nothing else like them; they dissolve so fast in your mouth that you immediately have to gobble down another slice to keep the taste there, and then another and another until you're totally bloated.

I unwrap Peter's package and find a yellow bag with a blue string around the opening and a hard cube inside.

"What's that?" Carol asks with a lump of sugar clenched between her teeth.

"It's called a laughing bag," I say, delighted. Peter and I have been admiring it in the shop for ages; the poor shop assistant got tired of giving us a demonstration of how it works.

"What's that?" asks Mom. Peter grins over his plate of tart and glances back and forth at me and them.

"It's this," I say, squeezing the bag.

And then the bag starts laughing. It's a metallic laugh that starts deep down and rises, bit by bit, to a ridiculously high-pitched climax of a splutter and giggle. Then all Peter and I can do is burst out laughing ourselves, but Carol and

Mom just shake their heads with a slightly nauseated air, not even attempting a smile.

"That's really silly," Carol mutters.

Then the voice in the bag takes a dive and sinks deep, deep below to a *ho, ho, ho* and shows no sign of stopping. Peter and I are bright red in the face and sweating so much from trying to suffocate the laughter that we can barely breathe until Mom has suddenly had enough of this nonsense.

"Turn that thing off and sit down here if you want some pear tart," she orders. "Where did you get that thing?" she asks Peter, as if trying to find out where she should send me to give it back.

"Some shop," Peter sighs with a wheezing sound in his throat.

I sit at the table and start digging into the tart, but we have to avoid all eye contact to stop ourselves from having another outburst.

"You're so silly," says Carol, lighting a Camel, the sour smoke burning my eyes as it drifts across the table.

"Moronic," Mom adds in agreement, lighting a Kent, with almost no smell at all. Mom smokes only when Carol comes over.

In the end, Peter and I waddle up to my bedroom with bloated stomachs, leaving the women in the living room with their coffee and cigarettes.

"Wow," he whispers, gawking at the falcon on my desk in admiration.

"Dad brought it over yesterday," I say, feeling a wave of pride because it isn't often that Peter expresses appreciation or gets excited about anything.

"Isn't that the falcon from the ship?" he asks enthusiastically. "Isn't that Christian the Ninth?"

"The one and only," I say nonchalantly.

"Your dad is just amazing," says Peter, stroking the chest feathers with one finger.

"He sat with me here into the small hours," I say. "We hadn't seen each other for ages. He had to do a lot of extra shifts on the ship, you know."

"He's great," says Peter, but I don't know whether he's talking about the falcon or Dad.

It gives me a strangely good feeling lying about Dad coming in to sit beside me last night. Maybe it's because I know Peter believes me or has no reason not to. Or maybe it's because I feel I have to even the score. It's actually Peter's dad who's great. Every summer he takes his family abroad on vacation, and while Peter's mom and sisters sunbathe on the beach or go shopping, he takes Peter to natural-history museums, national museums, and zoos. His dad is even a subscriber to *National Geographic*. While my dad sends me postcards from foreign places, Peter has actually been *in* those foreign places with his dad. While my dad is out at sea, Peter's dad is at home reading Peter long articles out of the *National Geographic*. And while my dad is divorced and has a girlfriend somewhere miles away, whom he spends all of his time with when he's ashore, Peter's dad is tirelessly making more children with his mom to make his family even bigger and happier. Sometimes I think that although God was a bit mean to saddle Peter with five sisters that he constantly complains about, he was also merciful to him because at least he has a dad who actually lives with him and who's a *National Geographic* subscriber to boot. What more could he ask for?

"I know what we'll do," says Peter. "I'll borrow my dad's camera, and then we'll take the bird out and stick him in a few places and take pictures. Then we can make our own magazine," he adds. "Our own *National Geographic*."

"You take the pictures," I say.

"And you write the articles," he says.

"Maybe your dad can help us."

"We could call it *Nature in Words and Pictures*," says Peter as if he didn't hear me.

"Or *Wildlife and Nature*," I say, trying to play down the importance of my proposal.

"Or *Mother Earth*," says Peter.

Peter is always full of ideas that he can almost always make come true. But that's also because he gets help from his dad. Once he made a crossword magazine and went around the neighborhood selling it for the Red Cross. He thought it was a smart idea: crosswords, Red Cross. It was called *The Red Crossword Magazine*. And he sat there for a whole weekend with his dad in his office, photocopying the magazine and painting the front page red with India ink. It sold well, and he donated the proceeds to the Red

Cross. Another time he got the idea of making a dovecote and breeding pigeons and training them as carriers. His dad supplied the wood and chicken wire, and we spent the whole weekend in his garden making this big shed-like birdhouse for the pigeons to live in. Then we spent days hunting pigeons with a stick, some string, and a cardboard box, but when we'd caught eight of them, the cat went into the cote and killed them all. The cote is still there in Peter's garden. In spite of everything, it was a great idea.

We discuss the magazine and decide that the first issue should have a photograph of the falcon on the cover. I walk Peter to the door, and he says bye and thanks to Mom. When he is on the doorstep, he gives me his stiff salute and strikes his tough military pose.

"Farewell, Sergeant Stephenson."

And I do the same—give him a salute with a perfect swing of the hand and a stern frown.

"Dismissed! Farewell, Private Johnson."

Auntie Carol is still sitting in the living room, smoking cigarettes and sucking sugar cubes with her coffee as I come back in for just another slice of pear tart. Carol is saying she envies Mom for working at a clean chocolate factory, but Mom says Carol's the one to envy because at least she gets to dip her hands into the healthy slime of blessed fish, which is a lot better than the chocolate gunk she has to bury her hands in and the clouds of sugar that give her migraines. Carol has a husky smoker's voice, and it really suits her because that's the kind of person she is: a tough, determined, thickset ball. She suddenly turns to me and peers into my face as if she were looking for ringworm in a cod fillet or something.

"Well, then, kiddo, so you're thirteen now, are you? Have you started smooching girls yet?"

I gulp down the pear tart I'm chewing and my face sets on fire because I can't come up with an answer, but Mom laughs gently and Carol wheezes from deep inside like the laughing bag.

"No? Well, that's all right, boy—plenty of time for that."

I avert my gaze and swallow the slice as fast as I can. How can she see that I haven't started kissing girls? I might have, for all she knows. Or is the truth so blatantly obvious?

"Your genes are sure to take over sooner or later," she adds, squinting through the smoke.

"God forbid," Mom scoffs, and they both giggle at their idiotic joke.

I suddenly feel uncomfortable sitting here listening to them. They're just two stupid old bags. What are they poking their noses into my business for? Why doesn't the old camel just buzz off home? *Don't you have to be on the assembly line at seven o'clock tomorrow morning, old bag?* my mind yells at Auntie Carol. But I don't say it out loud. I just say thanks for the tart and take my plate into the kitchen.

"He's really moody," I hear Carol saying back in the living room.

"He's reached that age." Mom sighs. "But I've been so lucky with him, never have any problems with him. He's awfully good."

"Then he gets that from your side," Carol says (she's Dad's sister). "But it's the quiet ones you have to watch out for," she adds.

I turn the kitchen faucet on to block out their voices.

I have a double reflection in the kitchen window: two split personalities vying for power inside me. My right arm is against my left arm; my right leg wants to stand still, my left leg wants to run away, my brain is screaming, but my lips are sealed.

Dad hasn't called yet. I fiddle with the laughing bag in my hands and inadvertently press the button. *Hee, hee, hee.*

I keep a small shoe box locked in a drawer in my desk. Inside, there's an old watch with cracked glass. It stopped at eighteen minutes past seven somewhere, some day, and hasn't ticked since. There's also a tiepin. The silver coating has started to peel, and you can see the iron underneath. Then there's Dad's old pipe, with its chewed stem and yellow and green electrician's tape holding it together in the middle. There's just a tiny bowl for the tobacco, so tiny you can barely get one smoke out of it. It has a sour smell.

Then there's an old photo of Dad, with sideburns, in an unbuttoned shirt, unshaven, with a big smile and straight white teeth. If I sniff the box carefully enough, I can still get the faint odor of his aftershave, Old Spice. Or maybe I'm just imagining it.

And because I've only just turned thirteen, I can feel the tears welling in my eyes again. *Stupid blubbering!* my mind yells, but my lips tighten. I put my father back into the shoe box, lock it inside the drawer, and trigger off the laughing bag. *Ha, hee, ho!*

Then the phone rings.

I fly down the stairs in a flash, and my hand is already touching the phone before it has a chance to ring again. I tighten my grip around the black receiver, my knuckles turning white, my forehead breaking into a sweat. The earpiece weighs a ton as I place it to my ear.

"Hello?" I call over the racket and wait with a lump in my throat.

A distant voice roars something I can't make out.

"Dad!" I shout.

"Happy — birthday — son — how — the bird?"

These are the only words I can just about make out through the racket and screeching with the phone pressed tight against my ear.

"Where are you?" I yell.

"Middle of nowhere — broke down — old truck," I think I hear.

Dad! my mind cries out. *Thanks for the awesome*

birthday present—you—great—miss—you—couldn't you have waited one day?

But I say none of these things. I take a deep breath and yell through the racket as loud as my vocal cords will allow.

"Auntie Carol brought a pear tart!"

Buzz, click. Then nothing more.

"The line broke down," says the switchboard operator. "He's on some kind of a ship radio—he'll call again, son."

Another click and then a long tone. The receiver grows heavier in my hand, slithers away from my sweaty face, and slides back to its place.

Hee, ha, ho floats into the hall from my bedroom.

There's a nature program on TV, and I'm lying on the floor with my *Life and Creation* book in front of me, and I write down the things the narrator is telling me about bee communities. Mom sits by the sewing machine in the middle of the living room. Multicolored threads and balls litter the carpet around her feet like cobwebs. There she sits, sewing for someone, on most nights of the week, after a whole day at the chocolate factory, except the night she cleans the printer's place. And the sewing machine hums and plods along.

There's a pile of material she has to sew on the ironing board, and another pile of washing she has to iron. In the old washing basket beside her, there's a bundle of some really fancy material that's going to be used to make some really posh people's curtains, and the material is so fancy that it isn't even allowed to touch the multicolored web of threads on the floor. The sewing machine hums and plods along, and Mom sits there stooped over it, as if chained to the thing. She runs the heavy green material under the needle as carefully as she can, because you've got to get the hemline right first time around.

"The bee community is one of the most perfect communities in the insect world," says the narrator in her silky-smooth voice. "Each and every one of them performs the tasks he was born to perform. We can only marvel at the organization and diligence of these bees, who work tirelessly and slave away for the benefit of the others."

I write that into my book and watch the busy bees buzzing on the screen.

The sewing machine stops humming behind me. I glance over my shoulder and look at Mom, who is threading the needle. Mom is like those worker bees. She never stops from dawn till dusk. In fact, she's the perfect worker bee, and unlike her, they don't have to pay rent or make money to buy food. The bee sits at the sewing machine in her apron. The bee lifts her heavy black head, her antennae drooping in all directions.

"What's this program about?" asks the bee.

"Worker bees, mainly," I answer.

Then the bee looks sadly out of the living-room window and gazes into the darkness awhile. No matter which way you look at it, bees have the advantage of having no worries. And they're never lonely.

"The worker bee," she mutters as the antennae sadly dangle over her head, as if she feels neglected that no one thought of making a program about her, the sewing-machine bee, mother bee, chocolate-factory bee. Then she bows her heavy head over the sewing machine again and presses her foot on the pedal, and the needle zigzags through the thick green velvet material that is too plush to touch our carpet. I wish I knew who insisted on her sewing these yards and yards of thick curtain. It obviously didn't occur to them that she has to work into the small hours, night after night, to finish this job on time. Why can't they just buy them from a shop?

"Have you done your math yet?" Mom asks, looking her old self again.

"Yeah," I lie.

"Your lunch is in the fridge. Don't forget to take it tomorrow morning, and put all your books in your bag before you go to bed so you won't forget anything. I'll wake you up before I go to work." It's as if the sewing machine's eating its way through the material to reach Mom's fingers, so that it can grab her and gobble her all up.

I still have to go over my math homework once more. But it's my birthday, so I'm legally excused. Besides, there's more to life and creation than math. Would Mom and Dad never have separated if they'd been good at arithmetic? And would Dad have become a managing director maybe, like Peter's dad, if he'd learned the multiplication table by heart? Shouldn't I be thankful that neither of them turned out to be math nerds, because I might never have been born? But it's also because I was born that Mom has to slave away in the chocolate factory and get migraines and rheumatism.

I've got a dad in a shoe box and a mom who's struggling for her life against a famished, cannibalistic sewing machine.

Chapter 3

"Life itself is founded on mathematics," says the head-master, who takes our math class. He always teaches as if he were trying to rouse a washed-out platoon to victory in a battle he knows is already lost. Even though Pinko is the headmaster, such is his passion for mathematics that he cannot even consider trusting another teacher with the task of imparting the wisdom of this subject to us, his students.

"Mathematics is the mother of all arts, the basis of creation, and the nexus that keeps the earth and planets spinning in their orbits. Mathematics is life, and life is mathematics."

Then he shuts up and peers through his horn-rimmed glasses, his bald pink head glowing. His gray suit, white collar, red tie, and sparklingly polished shoes bear witness to his refined taste and form an impeccable equation. He is God Almighty and holds the work of creation together with all his sums and divisions. He has given humankind the multiplication table and theory. No one utters a word during Pinko's classes. What can anyone possibly say once the Lord has spoken? And he isn't really waiting for answers, just waiting for the great truths he has uttered to become engraved in our minds, like the Ten Commandments on Moses's stone tablets, so that we'll never forget his words. He takes a tidy pile of papers off his desk and starts to hand out the test we took last week. Peter gets a 7.5; I get a 3. For a while there is nothing but the rustle of paper and suppressed sighs and groans from different parts of the classroom.

The first two hours on Mondays are math; human cruelty knows no boundaries in this place. Pinko perches on the edge of the teacher's desk and scans the class. He never sits in the teacher's chair, always on the corner of the desk. Probably because he's the headmaster and therefore cannot stoop to sitting like just any ordinary teacher.

The red tie works in mysterious unison with his dappled-gray eyes and somehow magnifies them. He obviously isn't too happy with the results. It's as if we've deeply wounded him, ridiculed him even, by performing so poorly on the test. Just to spoil his chances of achieving the highest average grade in math in the country. Under his leadership, the school has scored the highest results in math two years running, and this class is about to ruin his chances of a hat trick. We have dashed his hopes. He takes off his glasses to emphasize his words and puts on that same look Miss Wilson has when she's teaching us religion, because, of course, mathematics is his religion.

"Let us not forget," he says, "that a good result in math is a good result for life."

The few who have scored high on the test sit up, erect

and proud, confident in the bright and prosperous road that lies ahead of them, while the rest of us sink our heads, full of remorse and despair, with no future ahead of us.

The school bell resounds in the corridor, but no one budges. In Headmaster Pinko's classes, no one stands up until he says, "Class dismissed." And we're not allowed to dash out in a mob but have to leave in a straight line, in a civilized and orderly fashion. He waits there until the bell has stopped ringing, glances mournfully at the glasses in his hands, and mutters, "Class dismissed."

The worst is over. At least I wasn't called up to the board. The knot in my stomach, that eternal dread of being asked to walk up death row to the board, untangles on my way down the steps to the playground.

All of a sudden I'm standing by a tall mountain ash on the school lawn and glancing over at the field where the girls in my class are playing catch in the mild weather. There's a strange warmth in the air. I'm too hot in my jacket, so I take it off to hang it on a branch on the ash tree. The girls run around, lightly dressed in the warm breeze.

Maybe it's because I'm thirteen years old now that I don't see just a group of strange beings with ponytails who speak an incomprehensible language and live for nothing but whispers and secrets. Instead I see a stunning flock of graceful gazelles, with beautiful eyes and slender, swift legs, bursting with energy and elegance.

But there is one who stands out above all the others: Clara Phillips. Are her eyes green, or do they change color?

They are like a running stream that reflects the sky one moment and the multicolored pebbles on its bed the next. Long black hair tumbles smoothly like a silent waterfall of sparkling darkness behind her. A long white neck and a soft spot where her arteries disappear behind her earlobes, right under the curved edge of her jaw, where I could feast my eyes forever. Small red lips, the lower one slightly thicker; those lips form the most beautiful smile in the world. If the other girls are like gazelles, then she's the giraffe gazelle, *Litocranius walleri*. The giraffe gazelle has a long and beautiful neck and extra-long legs. She has a thin nose and very mobile lips. Her tummy is white, and her legs and inner thighs are blond. She possesses highly developed glands, highlighted by tufts of dark-brown hair. I jotted all this down in my *Life and Creation* book when I was watching a wildlife program ages ago, and now I picture Clara in among those gazelles, running free and majestically across the African plains. At the same time, I feel myself turning into nothing, at best a patch of lichen moss on the trunk of the ash. I'm sure if she were to look toward me now, she would see nothing but the tree. I vanish into a void.

More classes come tumbling out onto the lawn, and someone shouts, "Boys chase the girls!"

There is a sudden explosion of screaming and running in all directions. Screeching and wailing, but the predators charge through the thicket onto the prairie, and a stampede ensues as the gazelles desperately try to find an escape route. I feel my heart pounding and the taste of blood in my mouth; a tingle of excitement runs up my calves and tickles my thighs.

I leap into action.

Then everything turns to slow motion; I run in long bounds, soar into the air with high jumps, and land softly again, scattering the gravel under my heels, making it spin in midair a long moment. I'm the fearsome cheetah, *Acinonyx jubatus*. No animal on earth runs faster than the cheetah, who can move at seventy-five miles an hour. When he's hunting, he quickly singles out one animal from the pack and focuses on that one alone. As soon as he comes close to his prey, his sharp claws flash out, hook his victim, and ground it with a twist.

Clara's black hair whips the air in front of me, and her scent fills my senses. I stretch out my hand.

The cheetah holds his prey down with one of his forepaws and presses its head down with the other to expose the victim's long, soft neck and bulging red artery. Then he sinks his white fangs into the flesh; the skin tears, and the blood spurts out.

I grab her shoulder with my fingers, and she turns her head, graceful and delicate, and for a brief moment, I meet her sparkling eyes, totally still in the midst of all this mayhem. And I'm all puffed out. She swerves, proud and strong, and changes direction; I've almost got her, but I trip and manage to grab her shoulder again just as my leg slips. Slowly, slowly my back plunges onto the gravel.

She glides above me in midair, falling closer and closer, her mouth opening in bewilderment, her eyes growing bigger. She lands on me, and our bodies are thrust together for one endless split second; black hair strokes my face, sweet perfume envelops me, and her long white neck gently brushes against my lips. I feel the artery, feel the soft spot where the artery vanishes behind her earlobe.

A piercing shriek breaks the sound barrier as she leaps to her feet in fury. She dusts off her white sweater and stands over me, breathless, as I lie there like a fool and blink. It's as if I'm reawakening from the sweetest dream, the magic all gone, everything running at normal speed. Far too normal speed.

"Who said you could pounce on me?" she snaps, glaring at me as I clamber to my feet. Her cheeks are red, her hair messy, with one lock of it stuck to the right edge of her mouth. She brushes it behind her ear again with a swift move of the hand and adjusts two barrettes. She's got pearl drops in her earlobes. I stand there like a night troll watching the sun rise, knowing that it's too late to run and hide. I've turned into stone.

"I—I didn't mean to," I stutter.

I'm about to lose all power of speech when she raises her hand and I see her white palm in the air and feel a burning sensation on my left cheek, long before I hear the powerful smack. The warm breeze is still blowing, and someone somewhere in the neighborhood is beating the dust out of a rug on a clothesline, and a rhythmical beat resounds between the houses. Or is it the beat of my heart?

The bell sounds across the yard, which clears in seconds as everyone runs back toward the school, charging through the entrance and up the stairs. I stand there alone with a stinging cheek and a blazing heart.

Chapter 4

Peter kneels and handles his father's camera with a professional air, adjusting the focus and aperture and pointing the lens at the falcon, which I hold high up in the air. The idea was to take a picture of the bird in flight. Peter is playing the role of the *National Geographic* photographer and demands perfection and no compromises, but my arms are killing me from holding the falcon. Peter wants to frame the picture in such a way that my hands won't appear in the photograph. After a number of attempts, he's finally happy. He nods with a knowing air, and the bird sinks into my arms under its own weight.

"We have to do everything in our power to ensure that the first issue of our magazine is a success," he says as we turn down the alleyway, our usual shortcut to Peter's house.

Back at Peter's, everything is in a state of chaos as usual. Molly, his mother, is walking around with his youngest sister in her arms but still manages to plant a kiss on Peter's cheek and say hi to me and how I've grown, although I haven't actually grown since my last visit here. With the baby hanging on to her, she butters bread for us, heats some cocoa, and sets the table. Peter doesn't bat an eyelid when his oldest sister comes yelling into the kitchen, leans over him, and accuses him of having taken her makeup kit and threatens to murder him twice over if he doesn't give it back.

Compared to my house, Peter's house is like a battlefield in a war movie, with grenades going off all around you. If there's ever a moment's peace, it's only the calm before the storm, and then all hell breaks loose again. And Peter, the sage, sits in the midst of all this devastation. Peter has all the levelheadedness of a man who has seen just about everything in life and therefore is never thrown off course. Even though he hasn't turned thirteen yet, he has the life experience of a fully grown man when it comes to dealing with the overdose of women in his daily life and having to repeatedly force his way into his own room, over barricades of dollhouses, Barbie gadgets, clothes hangers, and cosmetics, only to discover that his youngest sister has just eaten a stamp from his prized collection.

"Did you take Alice's makeup case, Peter dear?" his mother gently asks him.

Peter looks up from his cup of cocoa with a forbearing and questioning air. Does she honestly think that a naturalist who wants to be taken seriously would use lipstick and mascara? Then she sees that he's innocent.

"Tina must have borrowed it," says Molly to Alice, who explodes in a rage, storming from one room to the next and yelling, in search of Tina to murder her four times over.

"The mouth on her," Molly says with a sigh, shaking her head.

Sometimes I try to imagine that all these girls are my sisters and that Peter's mom is my mom, his dad my dad. Sometimes I even wish Peter would vanish for a while so that I could take his place. Because, despite all the outbursts that he's always complaining about, I don't think he realizes how lucky he is.

Peter is given permission to lock his bedroom door because I'm visiting. But otherwise no one is allowed to shut a door in this family, let alone lock one. Not even the bathroom. Maybe it's to make sure his little sister doesn't get her fingers crushed or so that no one can commit any atrocities on anyone behind closed doors. The only door that can be closed and locked is the one to his dad's, Jonathan's, study, which is right beside the living room. It's full of all kinds of books and trophies from his athletics days. Peter and I need special permission to go in there to read the books. And what books! Wildlife books, nature books, history books, anthropology books. If I had one wish, it would be for someone to lock me in there so that I could read them all.

Once the door to Peter's bedroom shuts, he exhales as if he'd been holding his breath all the time we'd been sitting in the kitchen, and walks straight to the fish tank. His tank is bigger than mine, and he's got more species. He even has a special incubation chamber, some kind of maternity ward for female guppies. He lowers the incubation chamber into the fish tank, catches the fattest females in a green net, and transfers them to the maternity ward. There's a shaft in the middle that the fingerlings lower themselves through, down to the floor below, to the nursery, where they can grow in privacy, undisturbed, without having to worry about being gobbled up by their parents.

As Peter putters around with this, I start thinking of Clara's slap and get goose bumps on my cheek. I want to tell Peter about it but can't quite find the words. I don't know if he noticed it when it happened, or if anyone did, for that matter. For that brief moment, the world was reduced to just me and her. Peter and I don't talk about girls much. At least not as much as our classmates do in the showers after gym, and probably in other places too. The reason being that Peter knows everything you can possibly need to know about them, and what might seem like obscure secrets to most boys are just plain facts to him. He has no interest in the debates at school about whether this girl or that one has dark nipples or light ones, whether she's got any pubic hair or started to use tampons. He's seen his sisters' and mother's breasts so often that a pair of breasts are no more meaningful to him than a pair of, say, knees. And he's sat through enough seminars about private female things at the breakfast table, when his mother has been lecturing her daughters on the facts of life, to be an expert on these matters and know them inside out. And therefore they're not exciting. But on the plus side, this knowledge has been invaluable to him in our nature studies. Naturally we've often discussed the copulation methods of various species of animals and wondered about the purpose of all those varied love games that seem to precede the act. For a long time, we racked our brains over the female spider, for example, who eats the male after copulation. We never figured that one out. Maybe sex just gives her such a ravenous appetite that she thoughtlessly devours the first thing that she sets her eyes on. That's got to be the reason the lovemaking time among this type of spider ranks among the shortest in the animal kingdom, something close to a quarter of a second. No matter how cautious and thoughtful they are, one out of three of these male spiders can expect to be eaten by his girlfriend. I'm not quite sure why I'm thinking of these harsh realities of animal kingdom life as I touch my cheek, remembering this morning's slap. Could I casually slip the embarrassing episode into the conversation without any direct reference to it? I think Peter would start moaning if I were to start talking about Clara, let alone tell him that I'm in love with her. How could I deny it? I love her to pieces and feel so torn inside that I could explode. Isn't love supposed to be something like that?

"Are there any more pregnant females?" I ask, peering into the fish tank with an expert air.

Bubbles gurgle out of a sunken vessel at the bottom. Two snails are engaged in a motionless race up the glass.

"Don't think so," he says. "The other females aren't interested," he adds, opening a little can of feed, which he sprinkles on the surface.

This gets an immediate response from all the fish, who

dash over to nibble at the flakes with their tiny mouths, except for the vacuum-cleaner fish, who stays still at the bottom and, true to his name, waits for the food to sink.

"How can you tell if they're not interested?" I ask, feigning no interest in the answer.

"Well, because if they were, they'd follow the males around the tank and bite their tails."

"Right, I see," I say, fixing my eyes on the snails.

"It's always the females who decide," says Peter. "Remember that program about the lions?"

It would have been difficult to forget the lion program. That was the first and only time I had seen a male and female of the mammal species copulate. It was actually quite terrifying, because for a long time I thought the male was killing the female.

"Yeah." I nod casually.

"Well," says Peter, putting the lid back on the can, "it doesn't matter how hard males try with the females; the females will never give in until they're ready for it. And how do they do that? Well, by revving them up for action, of course. It's the same story everywhere," he adds, examining the guppy females in the maternity ward.

"And the reason for that is that women go berserk when they're ovulating and will do anything to get some seed," he continues. "That's why they're the ones who decide when copulation has to take place. The guys just have to be ready for action when the call comes," he says, as if it were the most obvious thing in the world.

Of course, that's pretty obvious when you're talking about a fish in an aquarium or a lion in Africa, but when I try to see how Clara and I fit into this scheme of things, I start to feel hot and drops of sweat ooze out of my pores like suicidal lemmings. I can just picture Peter's parents: his mom chasing his dad around the apartment, berserk with her ovulation. They've obviously got all these kids for a good reason. But could that be the kind of thing Clara has in mind? Could it be that she's ready for copulation, and might she have chosen me to fulfill her needs?

The sweat suddenly turns cold under my shirt. Why did she choose me? I feel a heavy burden on my shoulders, pressing me down. What am I to do? What's expected of me? Am I a sex-starved, roaring lion, ready for action, or a wimp of a mouse caught in a trap? I suddenly opt for the mouse in a trap and feel a pressing need to be alone in private so that I can work this all out in my head. I stand up with some difficulty and take the falcon in my arms.

"Listen, I've gotta go now."

"OK," says Peter, unsuspecting of my state of mind.

Alice has found her makeup case and sits at the kitchen table with a big mirror, doing her lipstick. She's put something awful around her eyes, has her hair in a bun, and is half-naked, in a T-shirt and underwear. Two nipples protrude through her T-shirt.

"What are you gawking at?"

I look away and stumble into my shoes, half fall into the lining of a blue jacket in the corridor, grope for the doorknob, find it with my eyes closed, step over the threshold, and dash down the steps outside.

"Officer dismissed! Farewell, Josh Stephenson," I hear Peter shouting behind me as the door closes.

I come through the door with the falcon in my arms, my head bursting with irritation and strange thoughts. Mom sits smiling with the phone glued to her ear and glances at me with that look people have when they're talking on the phone.

"Of course," she says, emphasizing the *course.*

I go up to my bedroom and put the falcon down on the desk. I'm all restless and fidgety and can't sit still. Feel like going out for a run.

"Well, I mean obviously," says Mom's faint voice on the phone. "Sure. Sure."

My schoolbooks lie untouched on the desk, and when I open them and go over the homework I was supposed to do, I get pins and needles in my forehead. I suddenly feel sleepy. I yawn and stare into a blissful void that no thoughts can penetrate. Mom keeps yakking on the phone in the hall, and her voice carries up the stairs into my room. "Sure," she says, "sure." The sun shines through the window until it is veiled by a cloud. Two little flies have woken up too early. One of them is dead already and lies on its back with its legs in the air. The other is still plodding away at trying to break through the glass. He clambers up, falls, and starts all over again. Again and again, and maybe he's thinking, *It's bound to give in sooner or later.*

What's the point of flies? Some of them are born to nothing but a life on a windowsill, spend their entire lives walking up and falling off the same pane of glass, and then die on that same windowsill. Could it be that God created a special type of fly for windowsills? Were these tiny, subtle creatures really solely designed for the purpose of soiling human windowsills? Imagine: a whole species, a whole branch of the insect family, does nothing else in its lifetime. And no individual is of any importance because it's immediately replaced by another. So even though one of them falls and wriggles its legs, it makes absolutely no difference. Another will take its place. Are men maybe flies on God's windowsill? Does he sit like I am now, watching human flies scrambling up his window? And if so, can he see me? Am I of any importance? And why am I here, at this desk, in this house, in this country? Why am I the one who is here? And who am I actually? A boy from the west side of town? Why not an Indian, a Frenchman, or an Australian Aboriginal boy? Or a girl?

My mom's hand touches my shoulder, and the flood of thoughts in my head grind to a sudden halt. I turn to her, and she looks at me with a probing air.

"What?" I ask, brushing the hair off my forehead.

"Is everything OK?"

"Yeah."

"We need to talk," she says, sitting on my bed, scanning the room for dirt and dust. She stands up again to pick some dirty socks off the floor, sits on the bed once more,

39

and begins to talk, glancing up at the curtains behind me as if she is trying to make up her mind whether the time has come for them to be washed again or not.

"Well, I was talking to Ben—you know, my brother? Now, it's such a long time since you've seen him, of course; you were so small. Anyway, he's sending his daughter to stay with us, Gertrude. You should remember her—you played together when we went up north that year; her mother's been institutionalized—ah, it's a sad story, the things that woman's been through. Anyway, Gertrude is coming south and is going to live with us at least until the spring. She won't be at your school; she's three years above you—no, four—no, three. Can't remember now. Anyway, she'll be staying with us."

She folds the dirty socks together and then unfolds them again, stands up and walks away, chucks them into the dirty laundry, reappears with crossed arms, and leans against the door frame.

"Won't that be great?" she asks.

I obviously have no say in the matter. All the decisions have already been made, and I'm expected to give them the stamp of approval with a smile on my lips.

"And where's she going to sleep?" I ask.

"In the little room here," says Mom, pointing at the door to the room we use as a storeroom, inside my room.

"In there? Why?"

"Well, the girl has got to have some privacy," says Mom,

pretending not to understand the full meaning of my question.

"How old is she?" I ask.

"Seventeen—no, sixteen—no, seventeen, I think," she says distractedly.

I swing on the chair and fix my gaze on the dead fly on the windowsill.

"Why does she have to live with us?" I rasp out, and start fiddling with my eraser so that the lines on it twist and bend.

"Josh, honey, don't give me that whiny tone. Gertrude is your cousin."

"So what?"

"Josh Stephenson, what's gotten into you?" she snaps, which only angers me even more.

"Is she going to have to barge through my bedroom, then?" I ask in a rage, hoping Mom will understand that this is no small matter.

"Don't be so childish. You can't expect her to sleep in the living room. And it's not as if she's a total stranger; you're first cousins."

"I don't even know her."

"Maybe the time has come for you to get to know each other, then," she says, vanishing from the doorway. The case is closed as far as she's concerned. I break my eraser in two, glare at the dead fly, and hurl a piece of rubber at it. Racking my brain, I have a vague memory of a freckled brat with braces and a pigtail that she was always twirling with her finger. It was as if she was using finger language to let people know there was a screw missing in her head, which there obviously was and is. And now this freak is about to move into the room inside my room, walking in and out of my space day after day, some hillbilly girl from the middle of nowhere. And then where am I supposed to undress at night? Or get dressed in the morning? In the bathroom or something?

I'm too furious to scream, and it's probably just as well, because then Mom would say that I was just like Dad. Whenever I misbehave or am out of line, I'm told it's my father's genes that are to blame. So what, then, do I get from my mother? Is it the ability to swallow just about any crap and never dare to open my mouth when I am being treated unfairly? It must be. Mom never says no to anyone, never to that brother of hers, nor his family. She never says no to those extra shifts they lay on her at work or no to the people who ask her to sew. Always yes with a smile on her lips. Then she can sit and moan about it to Auntie Carol, but apart from that, she never says anything out loud to anyone. The nos in my genes must be from my father's side, and therefore they're bad.

Dad is no.

Mom is yes.

Maybe that's why they couldn't work as a couple anymore. I draw the blinds, close the door, and throw myself facedown on the bed.

* * *

I was seven years old when he left, six years ago. We were renting another apartment somewhere else back then. They had frequent, long arguments, always at night, sometimes until dawn. I'd just started school, and they forgot to buy the things I was supposed to have with me, a pencil case and notebook. They forgot it for a whole week. One day Dad came home with some empty cardboard boxes and started filling them with books off the shelves and stuff from the cupboards. Then he stuffed clothes from the closet into big black plastic bags. Then some friend of his came in and carried his armchair to a small van outside. During all this, Mom sat in the kitchen, chain-smoking and crying.

"Are you moving somewhere?" I asked Dad.

He stopped packing the boxes and gave me a long stare. Then he took me into his arms and ruffled my hair.

"I'm leaving," he said. "Your mom and I can't be together anymore. You know how it's been — you've heard the racket we always make. It can't go on, you understand? People who are always disagreeing on everything can't live together."

Then he kissed me on the ear and led me into the kitchen to Mom and closed the door while he finished moving his stuff. When the van drove past the window, I saw that Dad's pal was at the wheel, and Dad was sitting beside him holding a green beer bottle, which he was struggling to open with a key. Then the van vanished around the corner.

People who are always disagreeing on everything can't

live together. And as I lie facedown on my bed, six years later, it occurs to me that this is probably why she always says yes, and never no, to everyone: she doesn't dare to disagree—people might stop talking to her. And maybe I've got so much of my mother's genes in me that the yes comes out faster than the no; it squeezes itself out of my mouth in the form of a smile and lights up like a giant blinking sign on my face. The feeble no crawls into a corner, having lost the race against the yes yet again. It throws itself into the sulking pile of all the other nos that were never said. One day these nos will have to find a way out and will all try to come out at once. Maybe I'll stand up to my mom's genes one day and will have to yell for a whole two or three days until I've puked all the nos out of me. Maybe that's what has to happen one day to make someone take notice of me, at least enough to make my mother ask me for my opinion before she starts filling the apartment with brats from the middle of nowhere.

Chapter 5

I am like a lizard: changing color every day.

One morning I wake up before Mom. I am already dressed and eating breakfast when she appears in the kitchen. I've finished my homework (math, the little I can), written an essay, and completed my grammar exercises. Then I run to school.

The next day, Mom has to drag me out of bed because I cannot wake up. I yawn into my cereal bowl and am late for school, annoyed and frowning, with none of my homework finished.

But whether my days start this way or that, one thing stays the same. Each time I sit down next to Peter and glance over my shoulder to look at Clara's face, I feel the burning on my cheek. I'm like a piece of bread in a toaster; no matter which way I turn, all around me are the glowing iron threads that heat me up until I start to burn around the edges. It also feels as if my nose has grown all over my face and my arms and legs are constantly bumping into things; it's like they've grown too long and I can't control them anymore. My knees ache every morning and every night, so that I can hardly stand up straight. After school I pop out of the toaster and sneak home. I feel like every movement gives me away. If I happen to swallow in the middle of a writing exercise when silence fills the classroom, it's so loud I'm afraid everybody can hear it. And not only that, but that everybody can hear by the way I swallow that I am in love with Clara. The tiniest movement in my face can blow my cover. I have to work hard to hide those all-too-obvious signs of my love, the little things that will expose me if I'm not careful.

"You're not getting the flu, are you?" Peter asks.

"Why do you say that?"

"You just always seem to be moping lately."

"Oh. No, I'm fine. It's nothing."

Then we don't discuss it anymore. But on the inside I am one huge emotion. Or like a cage full of singing birds, and sometimes I can't fall asleep because of the noise they're making. Then I get out of bed and sit at my desk in my pajamas and throw my feelings out in a poem, under the protective wings of Christian the Ninth.

> *I love you so, the best that I know how.*
> *All that was before is nothing now.*
> *Tonight, in dreams, I'll be with you at last,*
> *But the night goes by so fast—oh, far too fast.*

I see her face reflected in the dark glass of the window, surrounded by moonlight that seems to weave into her long black hair. In her large shining eyes, under those curved brows, the stars are dancing, her mouth half open in a tiny smile, as if she knows my feelings and wants to tell me she feels the same. Then she puts her delicate finger up to her lips to indicate that we must keep this a secret; our love is in hiding, and it is only in moments like these that we can meet and show our true feelings for each other. Our love is tragic and happy at the same time, hidden away from the prying eyes of the emotionless mob around us. Only on the wings of a starry night, in the freedom of a dream, can we meet and walk hand in hand.

The first song of the morning is the Beatles—the radio blares out, telling me to hide my love away. I crunch my cereal with sleep still heavy in my eyes. Mom butters bread. She hums the tune but doesn't sing the lyrics; maybe she has forgotten them. She doesn't sing any words, just "dah dah dah" or "bah bah bah," and harmonizes with the chorus. It's only in church on Sunday that she knows all the words and sings her heart out. She sings louder than everyone else, and I just wish she wouldn't force me to go with her every time.

She's been manically slaving for two days, arranging the little room. I was adamant I wouldn't help her. But then she didn't even ask for my help and ignored me while I lay in bed reading.

Mom found a cardboard box full of books my father had left behind. There were novels, poetry books, biographies of old ships' captains, crime stories, and pulp-fiction paperbacks. I took the box into my room and started to read a book about a wife who hires a drunk private investigator to spy on her husband, but then she falls in love with the investigator and tries to save him from the bottle and wants to start a new life with him. I find at least two really hot descriptions of copulation, which I don't entirely understand because my knowledge of words regarding this act are as limited to me as knowledge of the act itself.

The morning outside the window is gray, wet, and windy, the splashing raindrops lit up by the yellow streetlights. Sometimes I take a long detour into the neighborhood where Clara lives in the hope of catching a glimpse of her. Maybe I'll follow her or appear suddenly from around a corner, quite coincidentally and talk to her for a while, although I have no idea whether I would be able to say anything—or what to say, for that matter. But I never see her. In my mind, I act out our conversations where I talk eagerly about this or that. She is full of admiration and a little shy and timid; I am bursting with self-confidence and manhood. Little by little I turn the conversation toward my feelings for her; I place my hands on her shoulders, look deeply into her elfin eyes, and confess my love to her. She blushes, searches for my hands, and squeezes them, and finally she is in my arms, giving me the most honey-sweet of kisses.

But when I finally arrive at school, boiling hot all over from my fantasizing, I see her standing with all her friends, laughing, chatting, and so sure of herself in her unworldly beauty, and I fall apart. My temperature drops to zero. My fantasy is as far from reality as the east and west borders of the universe. I don't exist in her eyes. I'm just an invisible shadow, passing by silently in the darkness of the morning and disappearing into the classroom and into my seat. And since she is sitting in the back of the middle row, I'm just like any other back and shoulders in her eyes.

It's that idiot Thomas Magnus who has all her attention whenever he wants. Tom, the soccer and gym hero, has everything needed to get girls' attention. It is unbearable how shameless and disgustingly free of low self-esteem he is. He can turn in his seat and look any girl in the class straight in the eye, do some rude gesture with his tongue when the teacher isn't looking, and the girls just beam at him. He is so funny! Then the girls go crazy and giggle together while Tom just smiles a confident smile. At recess, he's out on the soccer field and doesn't give the girls a second look. They stand and stare at him playing, all hanging on a thread of excitement, waiting for him to give them an eye. But Tom has nothing to do with them at recess. They're just an exciting pastime in the classroom when he's bored. At recess it's the serious stuff: soccer.

Nothing in the world is as meaningless to me as sports, soccer in particular. The only time I went to Tom's house, he didn't talk about anything but soccer, and his room was covered in posters of sweaty, muddy guys with their shorts on their heads, screaming for joy just because one of them had been able to kick the ball into the goal. Of course, these guys get loads of money for this, and that's exactly what Tom dreams of doing. He's going to be a professional. I can't understand how anyone can be interested in games long gone by which this team or that team won at one time or the other. It's a huge heap of meaningless garbage; everything revolves around a victory frenzy for a fraction of a second, and then the fighting starts all over again. All the running is for nothing in the end. It's like a desperate attempt to kill time, just to have something to do, rather than doing nothing. Tom runs screaming over the field and jumps head over heels if he scores, but sinks into a heap of desperation like a flat tire, hiding his head in his hands, if he doesn't, just as his idols do on TV. Tom's fight for victory is as meaningless as the fly's when it struggles up the windowpane. You could set the fly free by opening the window. But even though somebody would open the window for Tom and point out to him some other possibilities in life, he probably wouldn't understand what that meant. And as long as he's in my class, I have to accept that his masculinity, his attitude, and his fighting spirit will always win in the race for her attention, the one whom I love with all my heart.

I've got to hide my love away.

Chapter 6

There's only one person who hates gym more than I do, and that's Ari Penapple, nicknamed the Pineapple. He stands like a ghost in the school yard every recess, and he never does anything or says anything. For as long as I can remember, he's been teased because of his name and because he is so tall, but at the same time like a heap. But he never does anything or says anything—not even when Thomas Magnus, the jackass, ever the hero, is right in his face. Then Ari just turns around and walks away. His face never changes. I've never seen him laugh. If he's forced to answer some questions from the teacher, it's just a low mumble that nobody understands, so the teacher has to walk right up to him to hear. But what he says is almost always correct, and he is usually the one with the highest grades.

But gym is the worst for Ari because he can hardly run at all. And that's bad. He's big and heavy, with legs like an elephant and hips like a woman. And the gym teacher, Ray Axel, enjoys torturing him, ordering him to run faster, do more, jump higher. Once he made Ari try to jump the pommel horse five times while everyone else waited and watched. But Ari couldn't jump the horse; Ari wouldn't be able to jump a cat, and Raxel knows that very well. Ari landed on the horse with a heavy thud and sat there, stuck, five times in a row. But when Ari has had enough, which rarely happens, then he does what I find really admirable: he stops obeying, sits by the wall, and doesn't move. Nobody else would dare. But Ari is just as tall as Raxel, and even though he's the Pineapple, he can sit quite still under Raxel's scolding and his face doesn't move. It's like he's thinking, *Raxel wants me to jump, but I can't jump. He knows it, I know it, and he knows that I know he knows it. Now, I'll just sit here and wait till gym is over; I'll shut my ears and turn myself off.* And then he shuts his ears and turns himself off. Sometimes Raxel kicks him out of class with degrading remarks. It's the only time I've seen a change in Ari's face; he smirks, and I know it is his greatest relief when he's kicked out of gym.

I wish I had Ari's courage, because I dread Raxel. His name alone sounds like a threat. He's got a limp, and he walks with a cane. His face is made of stone and his voice is low, except when he's angry; then he shouts. Then it's best to lie low, but the trouble is, it doesn't take much for him to lose his temper. He expresses himself mostly with his yellow training whistle, which he always holds between his teeth. And God help those who don't understand the meaning of two short whistles and one long. Or three long and one short. I can never remember the meaning of his chirping. That's why I'm too late to figure things out, too late to run — late, late, late. Then he picks me out of the row and makes me do thirty push-ups as a penance — that's two long whistles.

But there's another reason that makes me hate gym, that gives me a chill and fills me up with anxiety thinking of gym, that gives me nightmares the day before gym, and that's Sandra the shower warden.

To begin with, I can't figure out why on earth a woman is a shower warden in a gym for boys. Surely no other school in the world has a female shower warden in the boys' showers. Would anyone hire a man to be a shower warden in the girls' class? I doubt it. And it has to be this woman. Why her? She doesn't even look like a woman. Maybe that's why. Not that she looks like a man, no way. She looks more like a ghost or a monster or an alien or all three at once. And I'm scared to death of her. For some reason, no one else seems to experience this the same way I do, at least nobody talks about it, and that's understandable — because this is something that you can't talk about with anybody.

She's not old and not young either, not thin nor fat. And there's absolutely nothing she does or says that is terrible or horrifying; she just herds us into the showers, turns the water on with a long iron pole, and orders us to wash thoroughly. That's all.

But there's something about her, how she moves, how she looks, even the way she does her hair, that makes me terrified of her.

And her face is the worst. It is pale blue, and her hair is white and thick, cut at the jawbone, and her jawbone is broad and strong. She always wears pink lipstick, screaming pink, and her lips are really thin, so she puts the lipstick on the skin around her lips, probably to make them look bigger.

And her mouth is so wide, it fills me with disgust just to think about it; the corners of her mouth reach far into her cheeks and turn downward, so you can imagine it opening up forever, like inside there are no teeth, just a bottomless black pit. Her eyes are large and round, protruding far out of her skull, so when she blinks, it takes the eyelids forever to slide over these glassy water bags that barely hang in her face. And it doesn't matter how many times I tell myself that no human being has orange eyes, still it's a fact that hers are.

This is a face that stares at you in your worst nightmares, a face that never looks away but just keeps on staring, not cruel or threatening but completely empty of all emotions, cold and unmoving. That's why you fear that a face like that hides all the worst things you can imagine, and maybe something even worse than that.

We are running, sweating, and short of breath and cram into the locker room, and I hurry to undress and get into the shower before Sandra appears. Tom starts to fool around, stripped naked, waving his willy, standing on his hands, snatching somebody's underwear and throwing them in the showers to the applause of others who are in with him at the moment and therefore get to keep their underwear.

"Hey!" he suddenly shouts, throwing his leader's glance over the locker room. "Hands up who's done it!"

Everybody who wants to be in with him throws an

arm up. The others fetch their wet underwear from the showers.

"Naaah!" somebody says. "Who do you think you've done it with?"

But Tom smirks for a long time and moves his eyes from one to another while they're all waiting eagerly for the answer, ready to laugh and shout.

"With Clara cute-ass, of course," he says finally, and the shouts and screams echo in the room with whistling and laughter. I, on the other hand, feel a cold sting in my heart under the boiling-hot shower.

"At least like this," Tom says, laughing and grabbing his willy with his right hand.

And the boys laugh. "Yeah, Tommy, really Tommy, crazy Tommy."

I've started to dry myself when Tom's attention suddenly moves over into the corner where Ari is turning his back to us, trying to dress hurriedly, the sweat glistening on his broad shoulders.

"Ari! The showers!" Tom orders, giving us a wink and flashing his big white teeth in a wicked smile.

But Ari is not going to take a shower; Ari is dressing fast with trembling hands; Ari is in a hurry; he wants to get out of here as quickly as he can. But Tom is on the move, and nobody stops Tom the Tough Guy when he's on the move, least of all the Pineapple.

Tom jumps up on the bench and places himself in front of Ari and is going to order him to take a shower, but something makes him suddenly silent and dumbstruck. He raises his head and gives the rest of us a wide-eyed look.

"Take a look at that!" he shouts. "Ari has pubes!"

The whistling and shouting is overwhelming when Tom jumps to the floor, grasps Ari's shoulders, and tries to turn him to show us. But Ari is immovable. So Tom grabs Ari's underwear, which Ari is desperately trying to jerk up his sweaty legs, and pulls them down. Tom points at him, giggling and squeaking, and everyone joins in, bending backward laughing, pointing at Ari. But Ari doesn't want to turn around and fights with Tom, trying to pull his pants up as his milky-white buttocks tremble and shake, but Tom pulls even harder. Then finally the mountain moves and Ari turns, rosy-pink with tits like a girl and hips like a woman, utterly defenseless at the mercy of the mob. And it's true: he has pubic hair already. And a bit more than that—he's really furry. He's like a mammoth between his legs. He snatches a sneaker and tries to hit Tom, who moves quickly to the side, light and swift, and Ari's awkward defense tactic, with his pants around his ankles, mammoth fur between his legs, and one sneaker in his hand, is just extra fuel for the screams of laughter. It's so good when somebody else is exposed. You feel so safe. Then you're one of the group, not outside it. Still, I can't laugh. I'm trying to get dressed before Sandra arrives.

Then the door is thrown open and she bursts in, shouting.

"What the hell is going on in here?" And in an instant all the boys grab their insignificant little bald peckers and run screaming like girls into the showers, but I close my eyes so I don't have to see Sandra's face.

She turns to Ari, who is crying now. "Leave me alone," he growls, and then he dresses, whimpering and sniffling. Then Sandra goes into the showers with her iron pole, orders the boys to wash properly, and asks who was teasing Ari.

I throw all my gym things into my bag and run out, relieved to have avoided seeing her face, and I don't slow down until I'm on my street. How did Ari manage to hide this for such a long time? It hardly grows overnight! He must have been avoiding the showers since this started. And now I understand why he's been smirking every time Raxel throws him out in the middle of gym! So he could dress without fearing exposure. Poor Ari. Not only is he ridiculed for being silent and shy and unable to move and his family having a stupid name, but he is also the first one in our class to have pubic hair. And a dense jungle as well.

I wonder if it itches.

Chapter 7

Outside my front door, a girl steps out of a taxi. She's sixteen or seventeen or something. She opens up the trunk and takes out a huge suitcase and a bulging sports bag. The cab leaves, and the girl stands by the front door and presses the doorbell. It's like she's coming from a warmer climate. She's wearing a very short skirt, black tights on her long legs, and open shoes with thick soles. Her dark hair falls over her shoulder, and besides that, she is wearing a black T-shirt that is far too tight and short; her belly is bare. On her arms are loads of bracelets that jingle when she moves, and in one ear is an earring that dangles at her neck and reaches down to her shoulder. The door opens, and she scrambles inside with all her belongings.

As I silently let myself in, I hear a fast-talking girl's voice chatting to my mom, telling her news from up north. You can tell by the way she talks that she's chewing gum. In between are greetings from this or that relative who sends their best and is really grateful that Mom can help the family in these difficult times. Mom occasionally drops something into the nonstop stream of words, saying things like "Bless her," and "Oh, that's no problem," and "How is she, anyway?" before the girl continues her stories with her giggles and sighs. Before I know it, my ears have dragged me to the kitchen door.

"Now, this is my Josh," Mom says happily. "Josh, you remember your cousin Gertrude," she says, and looks me straight in the eye with a fake smile.

The girl turns to Mom and corrects her. "Trudy," she says. "I want to be called Trudy."

Mom is quick to realize. "Trudy, I meant to say. Now, be polite and greet her properly."

The girl looks me up and down, and I stretch out my hand. She is obviously unimpressed. But I don't care. The feeling is mutual.

"Hi," she says. Her handshake is limp.

"Gertrude is going to stay with us until spring," Mom says as if to emphasize that I accept the fact at once.

"Trudy," the girl corrects her again.

"Oh, sorry, dear," Mom says, and I realize that this cousin of mine is already some kind of favorite. Mom never uses this tone when she's speaking to me.

I turn in the doorway and go up to my room.

"Oh, he's becoming such a teenager," I hear Mom say apologetically. I can feel all the nos inside me jump up and throng in my throat, getting ready to hurl themselves out in one instant. So, to do something, I slam the door behind me and throw my schoolbag into a corner.

Teenager. Is that's how she apologizes for me to strangers? And what's being a teenager? I know perfectly well what it is: it's carrying your mom around on your back over thin ice that's cracking with each step, and all the help she gives you is to tell you off for stepping too heavily on the ice. Teenager: that's having no one. The only thing I have in all the world is this bed I'm lying on.

I'm like a shipwrecked man, clinging desperately to his raft, unable to see any land after drifting for thirteen years on the ocean. Now my cousin has moved in, and my room will become a kind of hallway for her. This arrangement my mom has made must be a breach of some kind of human rights. I'm sure there must be at least twenty million boys like me in the world that have seventeen-year-old cousins. Somewhere in China or Africa, there must be a boy like me who has a cousin like Gertrude. So why does this necessarily have to happen to me but not him? And why can't Gertrude be a boy? Then at least I could imagine he was my older brother, and we could have fun together. But no; she had to be a girl. And it doesn't matter what I feel about all this. No, I'm just "becoming such a teenager."

The door opens, and Mom stands there with a warning look in her eyes and a stiff smile on her lips.

"Well, Joshua, dear, now we just have to go through here a little."

"My name is Josh," I mumble into my comforter, but she acts as if she doesn't hear.

Gertrude follows her, dragging her suitcase and bag over the floor. She gives my room a glance. Maybe wondering why this isn't her room. Yes, she's probably thinking just that, the bitch. She shoots a glance in my direction and sends me a cold smirk. What's the meaning of this? Is she making fun of me or is this how teenagers smile?

While they put all of Gertrude's stuff in its place in her room, I leaf through a crime novel from my father's library and sink myself into a juicy and horrible description of the methods of a murderer who stalks teenage girls. I read and I read in a burning rage until I suddenly become very sleepy. This boiling inner conflict that finds no outlet consumes my energy, and I fall fast asleep on the book.

In a dream, I'm fighting to keep the door to my room closed, but there's always someone who opens it up again. I'm becoming so mad and irritated that I can't control myself. I stack furniture against the door, going berserk, and stand in the middle of the floor with a machine gun in one hand and a double battle-ax in the other, ready to face whoever tries to get through my barricade. The furniture moves and crashes on the floor, the door opens, and I raise the machine gun, but it's only an old woman standing there. A tiny little thing, at least five hundred years old. She walks up to me and smiles, strokes my chin gently, and says something I don't hear. Then she takes my hand and leads me to the door.

"You need some fresh air," she says, and for a long time I stare into her friendly face with a million wrinkles, glowing with warmth and kindness.

* * *

I wake up to my own mumbling—it's like I'm gagged. My face is flat on the book, and a few pages are wet with drool. I sit up with a heavy head, confused, my hair messed up on one side. The door to Gertrude's room is open, but there's nobody in there. Then I hear something behind me, and when I turn, I see my cousin kneeling beside my bookshelf, reading the titles of my father's books. I put my feet on the floor and clear my throat loudly. She looks up and smiles.

"Oh, sorry. Did I wake you?"

"No," I say, and feel uncomfortable that she was sneaking around my room while I was sleeping. She obviously can't be trusted.

"Can I borrow this one?" she asks, and takes a spy novel from the shelf, looks at the cover intently, and chews her gum. When she's standing above me like this I notice for the first time that she has rather large breasts.

"Yeah, yeah," I say, and stand up from the bed.

She glances over the other books on the shelves, then glides her gaze to my fish tank and from there over to the falcon, Christian the Ninth, which stands proudly on my desk, staring at her threateningly with an open beak. It's like she's thinking how she would decorate this room if it were hers. I sidestep by the bed because I have to pee, but I don't want her to be alone in my room.

"Was there something else?" I ask.

"Just looking," she says, and goes into her room without closing the door, falls into bed on her stomach, swings her long legs in the air, and starts to read. I grind my teeth and run to the bathroom.

She's obviously settled in here as well. Makeup: lipstick, eye shadow, mascara, blush, face powder. Hair stuff: hair dryer, hair spray, combs, brushes (three types), shampoo, conditioner. Perfume (three types). Moisturizing cream (four types). Nail polish (four colors). Hand lotion . . . and then sanitary napkins placed shamelessly right before my eyes. Then I see the frown of disgust on my face in the mirror. This is an unbelievable collection of all kinds of crap. My mother has never, in her life, gathered anything close to this. But she agrees to all this as if there's nothing to it. With a smile on her face, even.

I pee with a powerful splash in the toilet, straight into the water in the middle so the stream echoes loudly against the tiled bathroom walls in protest.

Chapter 8

The church is a big building with high windows and a long echo. Every Sunday from now on, for a whole year, Mom is going to take me with her to church, whether I like it or not. I will have my confirmation ceremony along with the other unhappy children of hyper-Christians, forced to confirm the vows from their christening, when they were too young to even talk, let alone understand these vows. Not only does religion seem to me to force innocent children to take part in the silly rituals of their insecure parents, but the manual itself also seems to be full of nonsense.

There's a whole lot about donkeys, sheep, lambs, and camels. Even a camel that can supposedly get through an eye of a needle. What kind of a tale is that? It's just like all the other nonsense and only shows how little Jesus knew about sewing. He certainly never had to thread a needle for his mom like I have. Sitting on the hard church bench listening to the priest makes me just as sleepy as prying into the small print of the Bible. Mom, on the other hand, listens with all of her face and moves her lips like she's repeating every word the priest utters, or is she praying silently? God makes me sleepy. And Jesus is just like any other hippie with long hair and a beard where he floats in midair on the altar painting and Roman soldiers throw themselves to the sides like goalies in the World Cup finals. Jesus is a lamb, but still he's a god and also a man and a shepherd by occupation. How am I supposed to understand this? If he's a god and almighty as well, why necessarily does he also have to be a lamb? What's so great about that? Why not a giraffe? Or a camel, for that matter? And how can he be both a lamb and a shepherd at the same time? Finally there's a psalm, and the priest starts to fumble at the altar, but Mom sings with emotion along with the choir.

> *"Each and every time you think*
> *Your little boat is sure to sink,*
> *That sudden death is certain now*
> *When weariness laps at the prow,*
> *You cry in fright: 'Where have you gone,*
> *Who keeps the ocean's wave in bonds?'*
> *Lord, you're hidden from my sight.*
> *You, Dear Lord, are sleeping tight."*

Yes, the Lord is fast asleep. And meanwhile the people sit like sacks in his church, not daring but to keep themselves awake, afraid that as soon as they fall asleep the Lord will wake up and be offended and send them on the first plane to hell. Why do people go to church? To make themselves feel bad? And why does God demand that people come to church so early every Sunday morning, when everybody has a day off and wants to sleep in? Why is he the only one who is allowed to sleep in on Sundays? And why does the priest talk in such a way that you gradually stop hearing what he's saying? And why are these pews so hard that you get a pain in your back from sitting up straight for so long? Isn't God supposed to be good? My head sinks between my shoulders, and my back arches until my posture is the shape of a question mark. Mom gives me a nudge, and I force myself to straighten up again.

There's a loose floorboard at my feet, and if I press it lightly with my foot, there's a tiny creaking sound. I press down on the board a little bit and hold it there and wait for the priest to pause. Then I let go so the board springs back into position with a sound that echoes around the whole church; the eyelids of the Lord open a crack; can I wake him up? I press the board down again and wait for my next chance. Everybody bows their heads in silent prayer, but I bow mine to hide my yawn.

I hold the board down with my foot, waiting for a moment of silence to break so I can force God to wake up.

I wish I could see him come down through the church ceiling and talk to the people who arrive dutifully every Sunday, like Mom, for one more attempt to get a connection with him. God is a little bit like the shopkeeper on the corner, old Andrew. When you come into the shop and look over the shelves, you want and want and want so many things. But he knows you don't have the money to buy what you want—everything has its price—so he just stands there, tall and thin with his gold-rimmed glasses and the gray tuft of hair around his bald head, in a white coat like a pharmacist, waiting for you to put money on the desk so he can decide what you can afford.

You can only have three chocolate-caramel candies for that, but you want a whole chocolate bar, because that's so much better. Because as soon as the chocolate from the candies has melted, all that's left is the tough caramel that sticks to your teeth forever. And it doesn't help at all if you make a sad face at Andrew when you are just one penny short of the chocolate bar. No, he's just like God. He gives out the treasures of this world in proportion to your financial situation. Of course God needs to get something back, just like Andrew. Or does he?

Maybe this is all a huge misunderstanding. Maybe God is not in the church at all and has never been there. Maybe the church is the only place where *he* can never be found. Maybe he's just sitting outside, dead bored, waiting for the people to come out of here, for them to hurry back into their lives outside, into the bright second Sunday of Lent. Maybe he's right where people are after church, having ice cream in the sun, walking through the park, having a swim, or taking flowers to a relative at the old people's home.

Mom and I always used to go there after church on Sundays to visit Grandma. She lay in her bed with her smiling face, her silvery hair on the snow-white pillow, her big nose, and her bright eyes. She was always so happy to see me, and her old hands, with the soft loose skin, were so warm. She always had a small bag of candy in a drawer: white pyramids with red stripes. Then she wanted me to learn some old rhymes and to tell Mom about the strange dreams she'd had. She dreamed quite a lot. Before we left, she always made me repeat what she had taught me so I would know it by heart. I've forgotten almost everything now, except a bit from the rhyme about the months.

Twelve: the sons of time hurry by my face.
January the first, with the year in his embrace.
February has fields of snow; the beam of light is thin.
March: the sun is rising slow, but surely it will win.

When Grandma died, Mom said it was God's will. It angered me. It was also God's will that Mom and Dad divorced, said Mom, and nothing could be done to change that. Why was God messing with people's lives? Couldn't he just leave people alone who had done him no wrong? Why did he want my mom and dad to divorce but not Peter's, for instance? Was it because they had more money and could therefore buy themselves a longer-lasting marriage, like the hard caramel bits when the chocolate has melted away? Anyway, it didn't change a thing, although Mom went to church every Sunday on time and sang higher than anyone and prayed earnestly. Dad left all the same. Most likely God isn't in the church at all, and therefore he can't hear a word of anything they say in there. The priest takes a pause, and I let go of the board, which jerks back with a sudden crack and a long creaking sound that echoes in the walls and ceiling, and for a moment I feel that everybody is looking at me. Jesus in the painting frowns as though he's irritated by this disturbance and loses his balance for a while, where he floats in midair over the Roman soldiers who are ready to catch him. He's just about to fall back into the grave when the choir saves him from the fall with a heavenly song:

> *"Beloved father in the heavens,*
> *Oh, hear your children's footsteps meek."*

At first I think they're saying *creak,* and I hide my face in my hands so nobody can hear my giggle, but Mom jabs her elbow into my side and joins in the high-pitched singing.

Chapter 9

Monday morning and I'm taking off my pajamas when Gertrude opens her bedroom door and stomps through my room, half-naked as usual, and I'm barely able to turn away with my pajama pants around my ankles. This has become a nerve-racking situation every morning. I might have to start sleeping fully dressed. When Mom and Gertrude have left, I complain as loud as I can into my cereal and curse the two classes of math that stare me in the face from the school schedule on the fridge.

I stumble through the dim morning light to school with the shoulder strap on my schoolbag ripping my shoulder off. I've just arrived in the school yard when the bell rings, and I have to run like mad into the building and up the stairs to be on time. Everybody's already in their seats, and as soon as I open the door to the classroom, I'm met with the silent stare of sixty eyes. I blush and try to glide really quietly to my seat, but I bump into a table on the way and the shoulder strap gets tangled around my left foot as soon as I sit down, so the bag falls from my lap. I bend over to grab it before it lands on the floor, but I hit my forehead on the corner of the table and I feel the urge to scream at the top of my lungs. But I bite my lip and am completely silent like the rest.

The deathly anxiety finally subdues when Pinko delivers the homework in the second math class, and I feel how the tension relaxes in my body and trickles out the soles of my feet. Still I'm not quite myself. For example, I have no control over my head in Miss Wilson's class. It wants to turn at the neck, and the eyes are searching the middle row, where Clara Phillips is sitting, carefully sharpening her pencil or combing her hair over to one side while she tilts her head and writes in her book or raises her hand to answer a question from Miss Wilson. And isn't it just magical how the morning sun sends its golden beam exactly where she's sitting? But then Miss Wilson mentions my name and tells me to read down page fifteen. The letters are muddled before my eyes for a while, and I stutter.

"Read properly, Josh," says Miss Wilson, and I try to focus on the page, but my forehead is sweating and I speed up reading. And then my tongue starts to trip.

"The farmer said that these stories were fabrics made by historical women full of flies. . . ."

Suddenly I can't hear myself because of the laughter all around me.

"Silence!" Miss Wilson shouts. "Fabricated by hysterical women full of lies," she corrects. "Keep going, Josh."

I hover over page fifteen, sweating like a pig, while the class around me boils with laughter, waiting for my next failure, like vultures waiting in a tree for a dying animal to give up its last breath.

"Read louder," Miss Wilson says.

"That when these women were in the kitchen . . ."

"Eating flies," Tom mutters behind me.

"Silence, Thomas," orders Miss Wilson. "Continue, Josh."

"Preparing the food . . ."

"And taking their fabrics off," Tom adds. Then the giggling starts for real.

"Silence!" Miss Wilson shouts, and hits the wall with the wooden pointer.

On and on I read, down page fifteen and sixteen, in physical pain, until finally I'm finished reading and the pages are wet with perspiration.

By the end of school, I'm Fool of the Day, and I stumble home, utterly spent, under the heavy load of my schoolbag.

I'm ordered to go out to the shops with a dumb note in one pocket and some cash in the other. There are always a couple of old ladies whispering to each other at the fish shop. These little ladies from the neighborhood have put on lipstick for the occasion. They wear scarves of many colors, with a tuft of hair, rolled up on a pink roller, protruding from underneath. They're wearing pale-colored coats, and their shopping nets are made from real nets, like they're out fishing for supper.

"One fillet of haddock, please," one says to Mr. Penapple,

Ari's dad. But Mr. Penapple is filleting and stands there in a white plastic apron with the sharpener in one hand and the knife in the other, fencing with himself. He nods to Ari, who stands by the cooler and reaches in to get the fillets.

"Rather have two small ones, love," the lady then says. It's always the same story with them. Ari splashes two fillets on the scale, and they take a long time deciding how many ounces more or less they need, until finally it's, "I'll take the big fillet and the small one." And Ari wraps both of them up in yesterday's paper, under the watchful eyes of his father, who nods and smiles to the old ladies.

I buy a fillet of smoked haddock, like it says on the note, but I can't hide the fact that I'm a little shy of Ari because of what happened the other day. Here he is on his home turf, and here nobody would dare to call him Pineapple or make fun of him. Not even Tom. At least not while his father is sharpening the knife. And nothing could be further from my thoughts than making fun of him. I've never done that anyway — I just want him to know somehow that it's fine by me that he's got a furry crotch. It becomes him damn well, I'd say. But of course one doesn't talk out loud about those things. I just take my time choosing the fillet, asking him if he has another one, maybe a bit bigger, since now there are three of us at home, and I let him feel that I'm not in a hurry and there's no bad feelings behind my words; I'm first and foremost just buying a good piece of fish from him, as I would from any other honest fish salesman.

While Ari is wrapping up the fillet, I see Alice, Peter's sister, run down the street, right in front of the shop window, like she's being chased by the devil. But nobody is following her. I swing the bag over my shoulder and stroll homeward and am not really thinking anything when I glance into a narrow opening between two buildings, where trash cans are kept. There I see Alice, crouching, half hidden behind the cans, smoking a cigarette. I am so surprised that I stop in my tracks and look again. She has her usual war paint on and is wearing jeans and a black jacket with her hair brushed down in her face. And there's no doubt about it: she's smoking a cigarette. She inhales with such force that deep holes form in her cheeks. She takes the butt between her fingers and is just about to shoot it out onto the street when she notices me. The smoke curls slowly out of the corners of her mouth, and she stares at me without blinking an eye, until finally she closes her eyes, curls her upper lip, and blows the smoke forcefully in my direction.

"What?" she asks.

"Nuthin'," I say.

"Are you spying on me?"

"No."

"Then what are you looking at?"

"I was just walking here."

"Then go," she says.

I obey and continue walking down the street with the bag over my shoulder. Behind me I can hear a trash can being moved around and Alice swearing, and finally she calls after me. She comes out on the street and leans against the wall with her arms crossed over her chest.

"Don't you dare tell Peter."

"No, I won't," I say.

"Sure you will. You're going to do it—I know it," she says, full of suspicion.

"I promise I won't," I say.

"You can't wait to tell on me. I don't give a fuck," she says with a provocative smirk, as if smoking is the least of her sins. "Oh, get lost," she says, full of disgust, then pulls out the pack of cigarettes, takes one out, puts it between her lips, frowns, and lights it with a lighter. The look on her face is like she's really torturing herself and is forcing the smoke down into her lungs by sheer necessity. It's so funny seeing her do this. She's just a kid, was confirmed only last year; still, she stands there like she's already twenty-something, with all that paint on her face and a cigarette between her fingers. I turn and walk away, and probably it's because I'm so surprised that I shake my head.

"Why are you shaking your head?" she calls after me. "Look at you! Like an old man!"

"Shut up!" I call back.

But then suddenly she is by my side, tearing at my shoulder, turning me around.

"What did you say?" she hisses, staring at me with her eyes, so black from all the makeup painted around them.

"Are you going to tell on me?" she asks, grabbing a fistful of my sweater, twisting and turning it.

"Leave me alone," I say angrily, and tear myself loose.

"I can have you beaten up if you tell," she says, and I feel the tingling of fright from the tone in her voice.

"Beat me up? What for?"

"You just watch out," she says threateningly, pointing two fingers at me with a glowing cigarette between them.

"What took you so long?" Mom asks when I come into the kitchen.

"There was a line at the fish store," I say, and hand over the bag and the rest of the money.

"Supper'll be ready in a little while," she says. "Tell Gertrude—I mean Trudy," she corrects herself as she puts the fillet on the wooden board and starts slicing it up into equal pieces. The potatoes are boiling in a pot on the stove, and the steam is setting on the windows.

I feel like a visitor in my own home. It's Mom and Gertrude who live here; I'm just a delivery boy. Mom has changed since Gertrude arrived. It's like everything is now done to please her, to let her have some peace in her room to study, let her sleep in on Sunday mornings. Mom would never order Gertrude to go to church with us. But it's all right to order me to do all these things: go shopping, take out the garbage, peel the potatoes, vacuum the living room, fold the bedding with Mom, change the lightbulb in the hall because Mom gets dizzy if she has to stand on a chair, thread the needle when she's sewing because sometimes her hands are shaking too much, beat the dust out of the rugs because it's too hard for her. My cousin never has to lift a finger. When I arrive at her door, I've become so angry that I bang the door forcefully with a clenched fist. I hear Gertrude jump to her feet and shout. She rips the door open.

"What on earth is going on?" she says, holding her hand on her heart.

"Supper," I growl.

While we eat in silence, we listen to the evening news on the radio. There's a severe storm warning, and all trawlers and small fishing vessels are advised to dock before midnight. But somewhere out there on the vast ocean is my dad, standing in the machinery room of the cargo ship *Orca*, dressed in dark blue overalls with oil on his hands and sweat on his brow. Maybe he's listening to this broadcast, this very minute. At this moment, the voice of the news announcer is the only thing that connects us. Maybe he sits down and cleans the oil off his hands with a white cloth and is wondering why in the world he had to divorce Mom and leave me all alone in the turbulent ocean of life.

Chapter 10

Vipera berus glides very carefully from underneath the fallen leaves, long, thin, and soundless; only her cloven tongue twitches, her eyes cut in stone. Faster than the devil himself, she strikes with her jaw wide open, and the pretty little forest mouse is no longer among the living. It disappears slowly and surely down the throat of the snake. Its last message to the world a tiny twist of one of its hind legs. Maybe it's just waving good-bye. The snake continues to swallow and swallow, and the mouse moves under the glistening skin until it has reached the middle of the snake. Then the stomach liquids start to dissolve the poor little thing, or rather to change it into energy, as the narrator puts it, so the snake can continue to glide around the world with her cold blood and stony eyes and kill some more. What are snakes for? I lie on my stomach in front of the TV and shoot a glance at my cousin who's spread herself all over my mom's TV chair, which once upon a time was Grandma's radio chair. She dangles a long leg over the side of the chair, chews her gum, and flicks through a fashion magazine, turning the pages so fast that her bracelets jingle ceaselessly. She's wearing a thin but wide sweater with a very low neck and the precious short skirt. Her thighs are bare. We haven't said a word to each other since I entered the living room, turned on the TV, and lay down on the floor with my book, *Life and Creation*. She didn't even ask me if I wanted to sit in the chair, although it was obvious that I was going to watch TV. It's time to make her aware of some rules that apply in this home.

"That's Mom's chair," I say.

"Really?" she says, not looking up from the magazine.

"If she wants to watch TV when she's home, then she is to sit in that chair," I add.

"It wasn't labeled," she says, like it's none of her business. "Where is she, anyway?"

"She cleans on Tuesday nights," I say, and try to make it sound as if Mom has to work harder because Gertrude is now living with us.

"Cleaning! Christ! I would never do that," she mutters into the magazine.

I'm coloring the shadow on my drawing of the snake. For a while there's silence, apart from the occasional sigh and the sound of her chewing gum. Then she stops leafing through the magazine, and I can feel a tingling in the hairs on the back of my neck. It must be because she's looking at me.

"Do you have a girlfriend?"

The pencil stops in front of me, and the sharp point is right under the stone-carved eye of the snake. I clench my jaw and lower my head closer to the book, determined to act as if I didn't hear the question.

"Are you deaf?"

This remark is followed by a light kick to my right calf. She has positioned herself in the chair so that she can poke me in the legs and the backs of my thighs with her toes. Then she starts to chew on this joke as she chews the poison-pink gum. Out of the corner of my eye, I can see her black-painted toenails dangling over the side of the chair.

"Joshy boy? Got a girlfriend, huh? Tell cousin Trudy. Joshy Woshy boy? Girlfriend?"

Poke in leg, poke in thigh, poke in leg.

"Stop it," I say, trying hard to keep calm.

"Still a virgin boy, boy? No dirty thoughts yet?"

I climb to my feet, black with anger, holding the book, *Life and Creation,* tight to my chest, like armor. I don't realize what I've said until I've already blurted out a damn good insult.

"Shut up, Gert-Rude."

First the magazine comes flying in the direction of my head — an immensely thick catalog, as a matter of fact — and I duck just in time to avoid it. Then comes my cousin, full force, with all her claws stretched out, hissing in the air, jumping on me, knocking me to the floor like nothing and sitting astride me. I notice she's wearing black lacy underwear. She grabs my wrists, pinning them to the floor. This girl knows how to fight; I'm stuck in a vise. She's much stronger than she looks. I could possibly shake myself loose by thrusting my hips upward. But somehow it doesn't feel appropriate. I'm a victim, stuck in a trap, and it's a curiously exciting feeling that shoots from my head down into my crotch. Her face is close to mine, and her breasts, large and heavy, swing gently back and forth under the sweater so I can almost see them above the rim of the open neck. She hooks her long legs around my feet so I can't move except for my head.

"Well, then," she pants. "Want a little fight, boy?"

I try to break loose, but I don't want to get free just yet. Her earring is dangling at my face. I could bite it and rip it out of her ear. Her dark hair falls over my face and tickles my nose. I try to move to the side, but it's hopeless.

"Don't get too excited," she purrs, and arranges herself on top of me. The two hills under her sweater rise and fall, and I can smell the sweet fragrance up from the open neck. The smell is quite different when she's put it on, much warmer and sweeter.

"Now, I won't let you go until you've had a proper kiss," she says.

I react immediately, trying to break free, but she spits her chewing gum on the carpet and sticks out her lips, kissing the air between our faces. This is the sickest and most disgusting situation I've ever known, but at the same time so exciting, so exhilarating. I've never felt such a powerful tingling inside of me. It shoots down my thighs and out of the soles of my feet, on one hand, and on the other it runs up into my head and out of my ears.

She's trying very hard to kiss me on the lips, but I jerk my head to the sides so her kisses fall on my cheeks, my neck, my ears. I scream and shout and pretend I want to break free, but really I don't want to. This is so horribly exciting that the humiliation is completely worth it. At least for as long as she doesn't figure out that I'm actually enjoying it. She chuckles as she nibbles my earlobes and growls. Then the excitement is about to overwhelm me, and she must not realize that I am about to shame myself by the natural function of the male body in this situation, so without thinking I grab the last straw that every cornered victim is forced to apply if he's going to run free. I spit right in her eye. She howls with a piercing noise, moves her hands to her face, and jumps to her feet. I run like a cockroach, on all fours, down the hall, up the stairs into my room, then slam the door, turn the key, and lock it.

Panting, out of breath, I fall into a heap at the door and listen to my cousin's thundering noise as she storms toward my room, throws herself at the door, and shakes the doorknob. But when the door won't open, she bangs her fists on it, and the sounds from her are far from being made by a human throat. It's like a terrible ogre is trying to break down my door, wanting to tear me to pieces. And most likely that's exactly what she has in mind. I sit on my bed, trying to catch my breath. I have to get calm and figure this out. While the door is locked, there's nothing to fear. I stumble to my fish tank, open up a can of food with trembling fingers, and sprinkle the tiny flakes onto the still water. How many fish do I have now? It's been a while since I've counted them. Are there eighteen or twenty? I close my ears to the swearing and cursing by the door and start counting my fish. The buzz dwindles down, and my body corrects itself; everything is as it should be, my breathing calm, my heart at ease. The program was really educational and showed conclusively that snakes are the most disgusting creatures on the planet. They're ice-cold and slimy and don't have any feelings, no more than a rug. They are, in fact, nature's greatest blunder because they're completely useless but ruin things constantly for others. They murder small animals who just want to live in peace and quiet—wind themselves around them until they choke or else paralyze them with poison. Just like my cousin there, who has finally ceased the beating and gone over to pleading.

"Josh, I'm so sorry. I didn't mean to be nasty. Let's be friends, OK? Are you all right in there?"

I listen for a while until I feel it's time to show my cousin how noble I can be. I feel really good about myself, having shown her how tough I can get and having drawn the line in our relationship in such a decisive manner. I hope that this will teach her a lesson and that she will show me a little more respect from now on. I turn the key, and the knob slowly turns until a small crack appears and Gertrude peeks through, eyes cut in stone. I realize my mistake; my cousin, the snake, has not forgiven my counterattack. She throws the door wide open so it slams into the wall, jumps on me, screaming louder than ever before, shakes me like a rag doll, and throws me against the radiator. I roll up into a ball while her beating and cursing pound on my back. She fills one fist with my hair and clenches the other, but then a key is turned in the front door. Mom's home.

Gertrude looks at me for a second, fiery red with anger, her hair standing on end and her shoulder exposed as her sweater has slipped off to one side. Then she lets go, walks briskly into her room, and slams the door.

I'm lying limp on the floor when Mom appears in the doorway. For some reason I find all this terribly funny and start to giggle.

"Josh. Are you lying on the floor?"

"No," I say, and rise up slowly.

"Where's Gertrude?"

I nod in the direction of her room and try to keep a straight face.

"Gertrude, dear," Mom says, and knocks gently on her door.

"My name is Trudy, goddamn it, if you could try to remember for once!" she screams from behind the door.

Mom jerks backward, staring surprised at the door, then at me, then back at the door.

"I'm so sorry, my dear," she finally says, devastated for having forgotten once again. It would have been something else if I had screamed at her like that.

"I was just going to ask you when you have to be in school tomorrow morning," Mom says.

"Eight o'clock," the voice behind the door snaps back, boiling with anger.

"Then I'll wake you at seven, darling," Mom says, and then looks at me. "God, I'm tired," she says. "Aren't you going to bed, dear?"

"Yes."

"Well. G'night, then."

My mother drags her feet out into the hallway and closes the door behind her. Now I become a little frightened that my cousin will seek her revenge for real; maybe she'll sneak up on me while I'm sleeping. A sudden chill of disgust and excitement shoots through me. But nothing happens.

I sneak up to her door and peek through the keyhole, like a mouse peeking out of its hole to see if everything is safe. The snake sits all curled up on her bed, sobbing into the palms of her hands. Her shoulders are trembling, and it's clear she doesn't want anyone to hear her sobbing, because she grabs her pillow and buries her face in it. Then she falls onto the bed, and the sobbing goes in waves through her spine. Suddenly I feel like a bad person, like an evildoer and a thug. Is she crying because of me? Or is she maybe homesick? Well, who asked her to move to the city, anyway? I know I didn't. *Yeah, sob all you like,* my mind shouts, icy and remorseless, while I undress and crawl under my comforter. Sob away and then sod away back north.

I have a hard time falling asleep; I toss and turn and listen now and then to hear if she's still crying. But I don't hear a thing. I'm angry and sullen. I thought we were enemies and was starting to look forward to our next fight. But there's no fun having an enemy that you've started to feel for.

Chapter 11

In a basement room at Peter's house his father, Jonathan, is lifting weights. He clenches his short fingers around the bar, puffs out his cheeks, sticks his ass out, and lifts. Sometimes he farts, then Peter and I giggle.

He works out hard on the weights—on the bench press, with free weights, and with hand weights. Then he shows us his biceps and lets us feel them.

"Try this," he says, and gives us each a hand weight. We can hardly lift them, but we still try, getting red in the face and sweaty, then we burst out laughing and our strength is gone.

"There now, try to do this properly," he orders, and we try but give up.

"You have to work on your muscles, boys," he says.

And Peter tries harder again and again, but I don't bother.

Peter watches his father practice, helps him count the lifts, writes down the weight. Then he gives me a look of admiration.

"Man. He's got two hundred pounds on the bar!"

Jonathan used to be quite a sportsman and the basement walls are covered in photographs from the time when he was competing in athletics—running or gymnastics or skiing. And even though Peter is not as much of a sports hero as Tom, he's still no wimp. He is built exactly like his father—broad, strong, and stocky, with auburn hair and short, thick fingers and legs. They're like father and son should be. They're very close; they're companions. And to Peter, all this is very natural and obvious, since he doesn't know anything else.

"Aren't you going to lift it?" Jonathan asks.

"It's too heavy," I say.

"What kind of talk is that? It will continue to be too heavy if you don't practice. Go on, take it."

And I push myself on the hand weights, mostly so I won't irritate Jonathan and feel ashamed of being a wimp. Maybe he thinks I'll be coming here on a regular basis to practice, maybe he thinks I'm enjoying myself, here in the Sweat Hole, as he calls this joint, watching him work out and listening to him fart away. Maybe he thinks I'm enjoying watching him being such a great father to Peter.

But with Jonathan, it's always all the way. Since I'm here, I must take part in the lifting and help Peter change the weights on the bar, assist him in writing down how much Jonathan's lifting. Everything revolves around me and Peter admiring his strength, and Peter is about to explode with pride about his father's overgrown muscles. Sometimes this father-and-son happiness is a bit too much for me.

They're so alike, a bit proud of themselves, a bit better than others, a bit happy about being who they are.

"My dad was the champion at the hundred-meter around here not so long ago," I say just to balance my situation.

"Really?" Peter says, but doesn't take his eyes off his father.

"And wrestling," I lie.

"Wrestling? Really?" Jonathan pants on the bench press. "What year?"

"Can't remember," I say, and feel at once that this is not working.

"What's he doing these days?" Jonathan asks.

"He still works on the freighter, you know, *Orca,* the cargo ship," I say and fill up with pride again, because everyone has heard of the *Orca* because of Christian the Ninth.

"Really?" says Jonathan, but then asks no further.

"His dad gave him that falcon for his birthday," Peter says, and it's good to feel the attention finally turning toward me and my father in this sweat-hole joint of father's pride.

"The falcon?" Jonathan says with interest.

"Yeah, you know, stuffed," Peter adds. "The one who landed on the *Orca* last year."

"Oh, yeah," says Jonathan. "I shot me an eagle once," he adds, and farts. He seldom has any tolerance for talking about anyone other than himself.

"For real?" says Peter, looking at me wide eyed, and I feel my father vaporize from the conversation.

"When I was on the farm with your grandfather. Yes, sir, I did," he says, and sits up, soaked in sweat.

Jonathan also needs to be a little bit better than anyone else. And sometimes Peter is like that. I wonder if you only become like your father if you're living with him. Or are qualities like bragging and chauvinism inherited in the same way as short fingers, auburn hair, and puffy cheeks?

The door of the Sweat Hole opens, and Alice, Peter's sister, walks in.

When she sees me, she suddenly jerks her shoulders up to her ears, like she's trying to hide, but I pretend not to see her and start to look at photos of Jonathan competing in various sporting events. Peter gives his father a towel, and he dries the sweat off his face.

"What do you want, Alice, dear?" Jonathan asks.

"Can I go to the movies?" she asks.

"With whom?"

"With Linda," she says, and slants her head a bit.

"Who's she?"

"My friend."

"How old is she?"

"She's in my class, Dad," Alice replies, and there's a grain of irritation in her voice.

"I was just asking," he says, and it's obvious he doesn't like her tone of voice.

"Can I?" she asks.

"What are you going to see?"

"We haven't decided."

"Oh?" he says with a surprised look on his face. "How about deciding first and then asking for permission?"

"C'mon, Dad, we just want to see a movie."

"An R-rated movie, no doubt. Am I right?" he says, and stands up from the bench. "Don't you have to help your mother at all?"

Alice doesn't answer, but she's red in the face, and her eyes shoot back and forth from Peter to me.

"Let's go," Peter says in a low voice, and I'm grateful for getting out of this oppressive atmosphere.

We slip past Alice. As soon as we are gone, Alice says in a pleading voice, "Linda doesn't have to help her mother all the time."

And then her father starts to bellow in a thundering voice, "Well! You're not Linda, young lady! And you're the oldest; you've got responsibilities. I'm not having you wandering off to see goodness knows what kind of movie with some girl we've never met. You've got to earn our trust by shouldering your responsibilities at home."

I follow Peter through the laundry room, and he doesn't say a word but is silent until we reach the stairs.

"I have to do my homework," he says.

"Me too," I say.

And for the first time Peter drops our usual salute.

"See you later" is all he says, then he runs up the stairs.

When I walk past the house, I can hear Jonathan's harsh voice out of the small window of the Sweat Hole, and in between, Alice, shrieking in protest, obviously not going to the movies tonight.

Chapter 12

"It's the seven o'clock news," says the radio on the kitchen table as Mom runs around preparing my school lunch and getting herself ready for work. I have an uncontrollable morning stare. I'm not really here or there. The cornflakes in the bowl before me are like yellow icebergs in a milky-white ocean, floating aimlessly until I drip the milk off the spoon onto the flakes and they sink.

"Heavy storms have continued through the night off the coast. After an eight-hour period of no communication with the shipping vessel *Orca*, we have finally made contact and learned of an extraordinary story from two of the ship's crew," says the announcer at the moment the last flake sinks into the milk. Mom appears in the doorway with her furry hat on, half clad in her coat, with a boot on one foot.

"Second mate Brian Gibbs narrowly escaped death last night when two loose containers on board the cargo ship *Orca* were swept loose in the storms, trapping the man who was attempting to secure the containers. Fellow worker Oliver Stephenson suffered minor injuries rescuing his trapped colleague."

"Jesus Christ," Mom breathes. She sits down at the table and turns the volume up.

"Brian Gibbs was airlifted to the hospital early this morning with severe injuries to both legs. Doctors say he is likely to lose them due to the severity of the damage sustained. The other man is said to be in stable condition and will remain on board the ship."

Mom is dumbstruck. And suddenly I realize that my father's life is in danger. Alone, standing on the wet deck of a rolling giant in the ocean, surrounded by many thousands of tons of thick steel with containers crashing and sliding all around him. At any moment, what happened to that man, could happen to Dad.

Mom stands up to finish putting on her coat and the other boot, but she's not in a hurry anymore. She wraps the foil around my sandwich and puts it on the table.

"Don't be too late, my dear," she says, and strokes my hair. "We should thank God that he's safe. I'm sure we'll hear more news soon."

Then she's gone to the chocolate factory. That's her fight with the elements. But that's never mentioned in the news.

I can picture the whole thing before my eyes: the gigantic cargo ship cuts the black waves, the white foam spraying in all directions, the ship rolling to the sides, almost capsizing. And the men on board, what are their thoughts? Closed up inside walls of steel out in the vast ocean? Their wives and children? Am I in his thoughts?

* * *

I sit next to Peter, and he taps my arm, asking, "Did you bring it?" I nod and show him inside my schoolbag, where the laughing bag awaits being tickled at lunchtime. But I'm feeling strangely upset inside and can't wait for the day to end. I'm like my mom is sometimes; I have to take a deep breath every now and then and exhale slowly. Once in a while, I manage to take a glimpse at Clara, who's sitting there so still and tidy and smart and beautiful and dedicated, so calm and lovely and at ease. I feel so small and hopeless. My head fills with fog and I can't concentrate and I'm completely startled when Miss Wilson asks me what Ghana's main export is.

"Cocoa?" I guess after a short while.

"No, Josh Stephenson, it's not cocoa, and you should know that."

Then Clara raises her hand, and Miss Wilson points at her. She lowers her arm, clears her throat a little, pulls the sleeve on her sweater over the back of her hand a tiny bit.

"It's cotton," she says.

"Correct," says Miss Johnson.

And I disappear into the fog again and can't find my way back until lunchtime, when Peter wants to give the laughing bag the stage. He stuffs it under his sweater and walks to the back of the classroom while everybody's eating lunch. Miss Wilson is reading the paper at the front. Suddenly a metallic voice echoes out into the classroom: *Ho, ho, ho!* Everybody jumps, surprised, and looks around not realizing where the voice is coming from. *Hee, hee, hee,* the bag cries, and then some people start to laugh and spit out their lunches, and before I know it, all hell breaks loose and the class is screaming with laughter. *Ha, ha, ha*—the bag can hardly catch its breath, either, and hisses, almost out of air with almost no voice at all for a while until it starts to neigh: *Hehehehohoho,* in a deep male voice. Peter walks around the classroom, moving his mouth in accordance with the sounds from the bag so it looks as if he's really making them.

Miss Wilson is not laughing. Finally she's had enough and orders Peter to stop this at once.

At last it's Religious Education, the last class of the day. And because Easter is getting close, Miss Wilson says we will read about the Last Supper. She starts to describe the ancient Easter customs of the old Jewish religion to us, the meaning of eating the bread and drinking the wine. Her face becomes really holy and her voice melodramatic. She is a really religious person and has never been married because of it. Peter gets a note from the back of the class, and he looks over his shoulder. Tom is blinking at him. Peter puts his hand in my schoolbag, grabs the laughing bag, and thrusts it behind him. It goes silently, steadily, down the row from hand to hand until it reaches Tom.

"'Jesus said unto him,'" Miss Wilson reads in a trembling

voice, "'Truly I tell you, on this night, before the cock crows you will deny me three times.'"

Miss Wilson looks up from the Holy Book with the sorrowful expression of the Savior, who knows he will be betrayed by his friends. Her voice is almost breaking into a sob when she looks over the classroom. The silence is paralyzed and holy.

"And how did Peter reply?" she asks the class, but nobody says a word, because nobody knows what he said. There is a moment of silence, but then the sudden answer echoes around the classroom with a powerful metallic voice, as if from the heavens: *Ho hee ho hee, ho ho hee!*

Miss Wilson is struck by lightning as the class explodes into hysterical laughter. Tom tries, in vain, to turn off the heavenly message, but he can't seem to find the button.

Ha hee ha hee ha hee ha ho ho!

"Silence!" Miss Wilson screams as she storms between the tables in the direction of poor Tom, who isn't sure anymore whether to laugh or cry but can't quite stop laughing. She tears the laughing bag from his hands, and it suddenly stops, as if it's aware that in the hands of Miss Wilson, it's wiser to keep quiet. Then she walks briskly up to the teacher's desk, then to the window, and opens it. The class falls silent and catches its breath in perfect unison. Miss Wilson gives us a victorious smile, as if she's thinking, *He who laughs last, laughs best.* She puts her hand holding the bag out of the window and drops it.

Distant sounds seep through the open window: a car passes by, a plane flies far overhead, then silence, silence, silence—until *plonk,* the bag hits the pavement below. But before Miss Wilson can close the window, the bag's last words can be heard roaring and echoing around the school yard: *Aaaa ha ha ha ha ha ha ha ha ha ha! And the classroom explodes.

Chapter 13

My father is a hero, returning to harbor today with the rest of *Orca*'s crew.

I get off the bus and stroll around on the cargo docks, hoping to see him by chance. I don't know if he's gone already and don't have the nerve to go on board and ask. I'm going to make it look like I've just been taking a stroll, like any other day, like in the old days with Dad, before he moved out.

We used to wake up early and walk down to the harbor and talk to the old guys in the small fishing boats who were cleaning their nets or just arriving at the docks. Or we'd go on board a trawler where Dad knew somebody he wanted to see. We'd sit chatting with other shipmates or machinists or sailors and Dad would have a coffee with something strong in it, but I'd have a root beer and some chocolate cookies. Then we'd go to the harbor café to meet some more old guys, and maybe have a donut or a sandwich. And the old guys always had this smell about them, of salt and seaweed and oil and tobacco. Sometimes Dad had some tobacco, and sometimes we got fresh haddock to take home with us to Mom. She would always boil it for us and we'd eat it with boiled potatoes and melted butter. And although Mom always put tomatoes or cucumbers on the table, we would never have them with it, because haddock is best on its own, Dad used to say.

Three men step off the cargo ship. One is wearing a long gray overcoat, with black pants and a white sweater underneath. That's my dad. I turn away and pretend I'm looking at the ships. They come closer, and I can hear their voices and their footsteps on the wooden dock, and then I look up to him. He doesn't notice me, maybe thinking this is just some boy looking at the ships.

So I say, "Dad?"

They stop all at once and look at me, and for a moment, it's as if he doesn't recognize me, then he smiles.

"Josh!" he says, and comes to me and embraces me. The smell of Old Spice fills my lungs. His sweater has just been washed and smells of soap.

"What are you doing here?" he asks, surprised but still smiling.

"Just, you know, looking at the ships."

"Well, what do you know? This is my son," he says to the others, and they say, "Hello," but then they stand there waiting, as if they want him to go with them. He asks if I'm doing anything special and I say, "No."

"I'll meet you later," he says to his mates, and Dad and I stroll the dock in the direction of the center of town.

I want to hold his hand, but it's too childish. I want to know all about what happened, but it's too silly to ask. I want to tell him how proud I am, but I can't. Instead I stick my hands deep into my pockets.

We stroll up the main street. The weather is calm, a drizzle of rain now and then. Dad is chatting about how mild this winter has been, and I agree. Then he asks how I'm doing at school and I say just fine and he asks how I'm doing in this subject or the other, but when I tell him that I'm not very good at arithmetic he says that's not good enough, that I must work harder at it, and I agree completely. Then we don't talk anymore but just walk, and he asks me if I want to come with him to the grand old hotel on the waterfront so we can have a bite to eat and I say sure and we go into the hotel and we take a seat at a table in the bar. He orders some coffee and asks what I'd like to have, maybe waffles and whipped cream? I say sure and he orders some waffles and hot chocolate for me and lights a cigar. And because there's just the two of us there and the weather is so fine outside and the hotel bar is almost empty and the waffles taste so great with whipped cream and jam and the fragrance of the cigar is so sweet, I start to tell him that sometimes there's some fighting at school, that occasionally I get in a fight. He looks a little surprised.

"Really?" he says.

And I tell him that Tom is constantly picking a fight with me and there's nothing else to do but beat him up a bit, just to get some peace.

"I see," he says.

But then this blissful moment sort of goes a little bit

to my head. The fragrance of the cigar smoke and his aftershave, his voice in my ears, and I start to tell him about how three big boys followed me home after school and were going to beat me up so badly that I wouldn't be able to walk again.

"It was the day you were mentioned on the news," I say.

"Really," he says.

"So I just told them that my dad was the machinist on *Orca*, and if they were going to beat me up, they'd better be careful. And guess what? They didn't dare to touch me! Didn't dare to come any closer but just limped away with their tails between their legs."

"Really?" he says and takes a puff from the cigar. "What does your mother say about your fighting?"

"Nuthin'," I say. "I'm not fighting all the time, but then I usually win."

"Well, that's good," he says. "More waffles?"

"Please," I say, utterly happy and completely bursting with joy, but I try not to show it and keep cool like him, looking around me uninterested, sucking bits of waffles from between my teeth by putting the tip of my tongue up against my right eyetooth, curling my upper lip, and making a sharp short sucking noise like he does. Then a new serving of waffles is brought to the table and I have some more, although I've had more than enough, but I notice he slides his wristwatch from under his coat sleeve and gives it a glance. Then my heart starts to beat faster in my chest.

"Well, Josh, son," he says. "It was so good to see you."

"Are you leaving?"

"Um, yeah, I was going to meet my mates for a while," he says, and puts his cigar down on the ashtray.

"But I haven't finished," I say apologetically.

"You just take your time and finish up, OK?"

He stands up and I have my mouth full and my face is sweating from all the hot chocolate, but he bends down and kisses me on the cheek and pats my head and I can barely swallow the mouthful to ask when the ship will leave.

"Not for a week, at least."

"Will you be staying at Auntie Carol's?"

"N-No, I'll be going to the country in the morning to Suzy, my girlfriend."

"Really?" I say.

"Yeah," he says, and buttons his coat. "But I'll call you very soon," he says, and smiles. "All right?"

"Yeah."

"All right, my boy. Good-bye, now."

He turns away and walks to the door, but I stare at the heap of waffles in front of me and the steaming hot chocolate, the jam, and the whipped cream in a crystal bowl.

"Dad!" I call out.

He turns abruptly and looks at me, stands still and waits with a question mark in his eyes, fidgeting with his watch.

"Thanks for the waffles," I say.

He raises his hand and smiles.

"Bon appétit. Bye-bye."

"Bye," I say into the empty hotel bar as he disappears out the door.

For a long time I watch the smoke rising up from the half-smoked cigar getting thinner and thinner until it disappears entirely.

Chapter 14

I wake up with a lump in my throat, and I really don't know why. Maybe I'm catching a cold. There's darkness all around, but when I turn on my bedside lamp, I hear my mom is already up, listening to the radio.

She bids me good morning with a happy voice and gives my chin a quick stroke with her hand and suddenly I feel the urge to hug her, but then she has stood up from the kitchen table. Somehow I don't have any appetite, but stare at the picture on the cereal box.

"Right," Mom says briskly as she starts to slice the bread for my lunch, humming joyfully to herself. She slices the cheese and puts it on the bread, all the while humming along to the music on the radio. She looks at me over her shoulder.

"Do you need a bowl?" she asks, and opens the cupboard. She gets a bowl and a spoon out and puts them in front of me.

"I'm getting a sore throat," I say. "I don't want anything."

She comes to me and puts her hand on my forehead for a moment, and I close my eyes.

"You don't have a fever," she says. "Have some hot chocolate." She pours some milk into a small pot, puts it on the stove, and turns up the heat.

"Watch the milk, dear," she says, and wraps my sandwich in foil, goes into the hallway, and puts on her coat and her boots. I'm standing by the stove, watching the milk get warmer until it rises up to the brim of the pot. I pour it carefully into a large cup, add three spoons of cocoa, and stir. I hear Gertrude say good-bye to Mom and go out the door, but Mom comes back into the kitchen and strokes my hair and kisses me good-bye and then she's gone.

I wanted to tell her that I met Dad yesterday, but I didn't. She probably would have turned all sullen and strange and silent, tightened her lips, and gone to work with a heavy cloud over her head. Anyway, I didn't have to tell her; you don't have to tell your mom everything. But still, I wanted her to have found my forehead warm and told me to stay at home today. I wish she would have. Somehow I'm so small on the inside, small and weak and vulnerable. The world out there is so cold and dark and gloomy, so unfriendly. There's a buzz in my head, a knot in my stomach, and somehow I'm afraid that something terrible is going to happen.

In the bathroom, I roll up my towel, take clean sweatpants, T-shirt, and socks off the line over the tub, and put them in my bag. My cousin has left a complete mess in here. The air is full of chemicals that blend with her perfume; the shelf is covered with lipstick, mascara, eyeliner, barrettes, and hair rollers. It's like a steel container has just crashed into the building and everything has fallen all over the place. On the floor is a wet towel, and another one has been thrown over the toilet. I pick the one on the toilet up with two fingers and put it aside. Then I pee with full force and make the stream go around and around into the water below. But then I look down and notice that something is not as it should be. Or rather, there is something more than there used to be. Some dust in my crotch? I bend over to look closer and realize that I'm growing pubic hair. Four, five, oh, God, no, maybe seven or eight dark hairs protruding from the skin on both sides of my penis, tiny, like flies' feet. The blood rushes to my face as I stare at myself in the mirror. Pubic hair! Fireworks, in all the colors of the rainbow, explode inside me as the faint radio down in the kitchen plays the majestic sounds of a grand symphonic orchestra. Pubic hair! I've become a full-grown man, and it's just a matter of minutes before a beard covers my face. Pubic hair! I will be working on the *Orca* a couple of years from now, with my very own Gillette double-blade razor and a bottle of Old Spice in my pocket!

At the same moment as victory rises within me, I hear that damned yellow whistle, blasting one long whistle in my head, and my happy smile freezes in the mirror.

The wooden floorboards sway and creak under our feet as we run around and around the gym. In the middle stands Raxel with the whistle between his teeth, leaning on his cane. Three short blows: run in place. And we run in place. One short blow: run ahead. And we run ahead. Somehow I managed to put on my gym shorts without anybody noticing anything. But after gym, I'll have to take a shower with everybody else. What will I do then?

Two long blows: push-ups. We throw ourselves to the floor and start the push-ups. For some reason, I'm not very strong today as my mind searches wildly for some solution to the shower predicament. Raxel's pale-blue sneakers with the white plastic over the toes appear right before my face. Then he knocks the cane to the floor right by my nose. Three knocks: everybody to their feet. We jump to our feet and get into a straight row, our white, sweaty T-shirts heaving up and down as we pant, trying to catch our breath. Raxel inspects the line with the whistle between his teeth, looks into everyone's face, and stops in front of me and curls his forefinger. That means step out of line. I step forward.

"Growing pubic hair, are you?" I think I hear him shout, but it must be my imagination. Probably I'm not sweating enough, not strong enough, haven't been working hard enough. He grabs my shoulders and turns me so I'm facing the thirty-eight staring eyes of all the others, so relieved that they're not standing where I'm standing.

"Are you a wimp?" Raxel asks, and at first I don't understand the question. But then I notice the smirk on Tom's face and hear the boys giggle and I'm speculating if I should answer "Yes, sir" or "No, sir" like a soldier in a movie, when Raxel shouts again much louder, "Are you a wimp?"

I'm sweating more than everyone put together and my lips tremble, but it sure isn't because I've thought up an answer or anything like that. I'm just staring at the bars on the wall behind the boys, staring into the opening that formed when I stepped out of the line. I'm wondering whether I shouldn't just step back in line and disappear into the crowd when Raxel screams so loud that it echoes in the gym. The boys straighten their bodies at once from sheer fright.

"I SAID, ARE YOU A BOY OR A GIRL?"

I'm just figuring out how long it would take me to climb the bars on the wall, open the window, and jump out when two long whistles cut into my eardrums: push-ups. I throw myself to the floor and start to work, but my arms are tired. Raxel makes the boys run in circles around the gym while I fight in the middle. Sweat jumps out of every hole in my skin, and that disgusting smell from the gym floor forces itself into my nose; it's so strong that I can feel the taste on my tongue: bitter old sweat, cheap polish, hundreds of years of sour feet.

For a long time, I sit on the bench in the locker room, waiting for the boys to go into the showers so I can sneak out. But they're not in a hurry. The accumulated tension from the gym finds its outlet in the locker room, and, of course, Tommy is the leader. He has nothing to be ashamed of, completely bald around the pecker. Nobody has pubic hair. Nobody except for me and Ari Pineapple. But he's not here because he's got permission now not to attend gym.

Why didn't I go back to bed this morning after Mom left?

When everybody's in the shower, I try to put my clothes on. But then the door opens and Sandra enters. I'm too late to close my eyes but freeze on the spot where I sit with my hands stuck to the sock on my right foot.

"Take a shower, dear," she says. The corners of her mouth turn downward, her eyes so big they're about to pop out of her skull. "Quick! Shorts off!"

I stare at Sandra's feet, praying she'll move away. I'm about to say something, anything, just so she'll leave, but my jaw is so stiff I can't move it. I raise my head with great difficulty and look up, but then Sandra isn't Sandra anymore. Instead of her head, she has the huge, slimy head of a bullfrog, with eyes as big as a soccer ball: *Rana catesbeiana*. Saliva drips from the wide corners of the frog's mouth, and it blinks, looking straight at me. Thick eyelids move slowly downward, stretching over bulging, watery eyes, and then rise again, just as slowly. The sound of the water in the showers and the chatting of the boys grows faint and distant, and every movement becomes horribly slow. The giant eyes roll once in the frog's head, then look straight at me again. The thin lips move apart, and the dark void opens, so the saliva dangles between the toothless lips, then wider and wider till it's fully open and I can see straight into a terrible dark, red bottomless pit, far, far down into a never-ending throat.

Then the nightmare starts for real. I'm paralyzed: glued to the bench. A huge, slimy tongue rises up from within the mouth and rolls out, stretching in a long arc over the room, closer, closer, until it touches my chest, cold and wet, and sticks to me like it's glued. I open my mouth to scream, but there's no sound except my trembling breath. The frog starts to pull me in; the tongue pulls and pulls and the skin on my chest stretches as if it's going to rip off if I fight the pulling, if I don't let myself be pulled up and into the dripping-wet mouth.

Then something snaps in my head with a loud crack, and a scream shoots out of my mouth. I scream with all the force of my body and my soul, and the tongue and the frog disappear at once. Sandra the shower warden stands over me, looking completely perplexed.

I'm still screaming, and the boys line up at the door to the showers with questioning looks on their faces. They stare at me and then at one another. I think I hear Sandra say something, but at the same moment, she reaches out to touch me and I finally get my strength back. I rip myself off her, snatch my clothes, and run out the door, out into the cold sun, wearing only my gym shorts.

I don't stop until I'm on the corner, where I pull my pants up my sweaty legs, and I can't hear anything and I can't see anything but I keep running until I fall crying into our house, throw my schoolbag to the floor, and rush into the bathroom. I search the cabinet in a frenzy until I find what I'm looking for: the tweezers. I pull down my pants in a hurry, stoop over, and tear away my shame, and with every hair I pull out of my skin, I damn everything and everyone. I'm out of their jurisdiction. I'm not a part of this anymore. I'm gone and I'm not coming back. Never again, never again, never again.

Chapter 15

I rest in the hollow of my rock, down by the sea, looking out over the bay. This my only shelter in all the world, a little hollow in a huge boulder, on the rocky beach. From here I'm invisible to the world and the world is invisible to me. In the bay, the distant island with the lighthouse, the oil tanks on the peninsula in the east, and the seagulls, circling over the sewage outlet in the shallow waters below. I haven't been here for some time now. Long ago, a great chunk broke from this huge rock and left a gap, which forms my small shelter from the wind and rain. If I get too cold, I can light a little fire to warm my hands. I can watch the clouds gather or disperse and watch the seagulls hang in the air. I'm utterly alone here. Nobody ever comes here. At high tide, the foam from the waves almost reaches my feet, but at low tide, the rocks below are covered in seaweed, decorated with different types of shells, far below me. The sounds of the harbor behind me echo in the air: trucks driving, full of iced fish in large boxes that slide on the wet surfaces inside; the steady beat of the iron hammer from the steelworks far away; the air smells of rotten fish slime and seaweed and the sewage pump, oil and tar, and the salty nets lying in heaps by the fishing sheds.

And as this chorus echoes all around me, as the fragrances of seaweed and oil flare up my nostrils, as the seagulls circle in the air above me, as a group of eider ducks rises and falls on the waves of the bay, the tears begin to roll. Why doesn't Dad ever call me?

My childhood has faded like a bright summer day in laughter and games on a sunny field under the blue sky. That day has now come to evening. Before me is the black forest of my grown-up years, full of monsters and insects and dangers with each step, bullfrogs, snakes, and poison spiders; a thick undergrowth that I have to fight through to move onward, but I don't know where to. I've been pushed forward and there's no turning back. I'm empty inside, like the curled-up skin from an apple. Is this being a grown-up? Or is this just being thirteen? To have no friend in the world, nobody who understands, nobody to take me in their arms. The only bosom where I can rest is the bosom of my rock. But I even hear the herring gull circling overhead, laughing at me and my misery. I wish I was dead and gone and would never have to see anyone I know. Why does God make all this happen? Maybe there is no God, no merciful Father and Jesus and angels and Mary. Is it all for show? Maybe you are utterly alone in the world. And when you die, you just disappear, vaporize, cease to exist. The herring gull glides over the rocks and laughs.

Once I read a story about a man who was going to throw himself off the docks and commit suicide, but then God sent an angel. The angel turned itself into a little child and jumped in the harbor, so the man had to jump in to rescue the child, and he decided not to kill himself. If this story is true, if God is really that good with those who are desperate, then why has he sent me a laughing herring gull? Am I worth nothing? Can't he spare an angel for me? Maybe he just wants to get rid of me. Maybe I'm in the way. He obviously doesn't want to rescue me; he just laughs at me and my sorrows. Is this how you clean up your mistakes, God? Eat the apple from inside me and leave the skin for laughing herring gulls? All right, you, I won't be in your way anymore. I'll disappear. I'm going to commit suicide.

A sharp trembling goes through my body, and my hands are cold. I wipe tears and snot from my face; my eyes hurt and my throat is sore.

I can just picture when Pinko, the stupid idiot, gathers everybody in the school auditorium; teachers and students alike stand silent and wait and listen.

"I have grave tidings for you all," he says, and the room is utterly quiet. Everyone senses that something terrible has happened. Pinko rearranges his glasses, and his hands are trembling; his conscience is torturing him.

"Today, Heaven is richer by one angel," he says in a shaky voice. "But we here in this little school have lost one of our most talented students, a lovely young man and a good student: Josh Stephenson is dead."

The sighs and groans go through the crowd; teachers bow their heads, and boys and girls look desperately at one another. Raxel covers his face with his hands, and Sandra clings to him in speechless fright. They realize they'll never work in any school gym again. Peter cries bitter tears: he has lost a trusted friend. And my Clara, she can't believe what she's hearing. Now she realizes that it was me she loved with all her heart, that it was me she saw in her dreams. But now it's too late. She stands up and looks over the crowd.

"You killed him!" she shouts, and points an accusing finger at Pinko. "You and your uncompassionate, loveless, cruel heartlessness! You're all murderers!" she shouts. "He lives on, yes, he lives on in the hearts of those who loved him. You can't get to him there!" Then she runs out, overwhelmed with grief.

Everybody is thinking the same thing: *if only I had been nicer to him, if only I had been more understanding, if only, if only.* But now he's gone and it's too late, nothing left but a black hole of guilt in the souls of the wicked, but a sweet memory of a good boy in the hearts of the others.

I tremble and shake from the exhilarating sorrow, the tragic ecstasy, exhausted from my imagination, from thinking about the impact my death might have on the world. But what about Mom and Dad? I expect they'd be relieved. At least Mom could stop working so much, and Dad doesn't care about me anyway. What the hell was the meaning of giving me a stuffed falcon? He is a stuffed idiot. He probably didn't get permission from Floozy Suzy, his girlfriend, to keep it, and so rather than just throwing it away, sent it to me.

The herring gull chuckles as he flies in circles high in the sky. He probably can't wait to pick the meat from my corpse.

In the cupboard under the kitchen sink, there is a plastic bottle marked with three crosses and a skull. Poison. Many have taken poison and died immediately, although I suspect it's rather painful. I kneel on the kitchen floor, unscrew the top, and sniff carefully. It's like a punch in the face. I jerk back and throw the bottle into the cupboard. I could never drink that.

In the kitchen drawer, the blades of knives lie side by side. They fillet fish, carve meat, or slice bread; they have this innocent look about them, in spite of their malicious potential. Their sharp blades gleam at me. I take one of them, the one with the long, thin blade; it could easily go through me. Maybe I lack the strength to push it all the way in or the courage to cut my wrist. I place the blade on the thin skin of my wrist and press lightly on the blue veins. The skin turns white under its edge. I get butterflies in my stomach as if I'm standing on a high cliff. I throw the knife back in the drawer and shut it.

I could jump into the ocean and swim out until I get tired, I think as I wander into the living room. They say that drowning is like falling asleep; you don't feel a thing. The curtains flicker in the breeze from the half-open window. The dim afternoon light filters into the living room, casting an eerie glow on the walls. What if my corpse drifts out to the ocean? I'll be like those people you hear about who disappear and are never found. Maybe someone would be accused of killing me. If my body was never found, then nobody would ever know for sure whether I was dead or not. The magnificent influence of my death on society is starting to fade in my mind. It's not easy to take your own life. Maybe I don't have to die right away, not today or tomorrow. Maybe the day after.

Chapter 16

Dear Mr. Pickard,

Because of an uncontrollable situation, my son, Josh Stephenson, cannot come to school for some time. I will see to it that he does his homework as possible, but due to a family situation, it is not possible for him to attend school. I do not wish to discuss this with you at this point, but hope that this letter is enough to explain his absence. I ask you sincerely to do nothing until I make contact with you.

Yours sincerely,

I print the letter from Gertrude's old computer and read it over and over, the letter that will secure my amnesty for as long as I care to stay alive. Now all I need is Mom's signature, and then I can mail it and not worry about school anymore.

I sit for some time at the desk in my cousin's room and look out the window. From here, I can see through the window and into my own room, my desk, where the falcon stands high, and into the corner where my fish tank is all lit up on my dresser. My earthly belongings are few and insignificant. Before too long, Mom will have rid herself of those things. And the only thing that'll remind the world of my existence will be a photo of me in the living room, in a beautiful frame. And every night she'll light a candle by that photo. But after many, many years, when she too is dead, then nobody will know I ever existed.

My head slowly bows down to my chest where I sit in Mom's TV chair. The dark-blue curtain in the living room by my side moves slowly in the twilight. I yawn. I'm tired and sleepy. It's so nice to let your eyes close by themselves. Maybe, if my sleep is deep enough, I'll never wake up again. I picture the obituaries in the papers, one after the other, with a photo of me and a small black cross next to my name. *Those whom the gods love die young,* they all begin, then everything turns hazy and I fall into the long sleep, without any pain.

Sudden noise in the kitchen jolts me awake. I open my eyes wide and jump to my feet as if woken from the dead. There's a buzz in my head, pins and needles in my arm, a pain in my throat.

"You were sleeping so soundly," Mom says when I enter the kitchen. "I didn't want to wake you."

I don't say anything, still half in the land of the dead, trying to figure out what's going on. Mom is making dinner. She skins the fillet with the knife I was going to stab myself with, cuts the fillet into pieces, dips them in beaten eggs and milk, and puts them on a plate with breadcrumbs and rolls them on each side. My head feels heavy, and I'm bursting for the toilet. If I'd dared to do what I was going to do, I'd be lying on the kitchen floor by now, either with a bottle of poison by my side or soaked in blood. And Mom would be crying her eyes out over my body, ambulance outside, doctor, police, a stretcher, and a white sheet over my face; the blinking lights would be falling through the kitchen window, hitting the white walls at regular intervals; red spots forming on the sheet where I stabbed myself.

But I didn't stab myself, and Mom is just making dinner. Potatoes are boiling away, and the lid jingles gently on the brim of the pot. It's already dark outside, and I watch Mom's reflection in the window as she stands by the wooden chopping board, cutting an onion. Fried fish with onions, potatoes, and a glass of ice-cold milk. It's like a reward for being alive. It was good to sleep. I feel better; I'm numb, and there's not a thought in my head. And the best thing is that Mom suspects nothing and simply hums along to the radio. I could sit like this all evening. It would be so nice to sit like this for a long, long time.

But I'm forced to my feet by the pressure in my bladder, and I go upstairs to the bathroom. For about half a second, I stand in the doorway and stare at the wonder before my eyes. At first I don't react. Maybe I'm not fully awake yet; maybe I'm still dreaming; maybe I've started to hallucinate. Up from the frothy white bubbles in the bathtub rise two firm, round, and glistening breasts. My cousin Gertrude has her head under the surface and is combing her fingers through her hair in the water. Her breasts are large and beautiful, and there are little wisps of lather on each of the dark-brown nipples. And suddenly I don't need to pee. Without thinking I sneak into the bathroom and crouch under the towels on the hanger, press myself up against the wall, and peek through a tiny gap between two towels. Most likely I'm still sleeping; otherwise I would have run out of here. But I can't move; I am limp like the other towels, watching. Suddenly her head rises out of the water, she catches her breath, moans with pleasure, and dries the water from her face. Then she notices that the door is ajar. My heart is not beating anymore. I'm no longer a towel, I'm one of the tiles in the wall.

"Betty?" she shouts.

"Yes, dear?" Mom calls up the stairs.

"Can you close the bathroom door? It's opened," Gertrude shouts back and covers her breasts. My mom's footsteps come up the stairs.

She takes the knob, and as she closes the door she says, "It does that all the time. You'd better just lock it next time." Then she closes the door tightly.

My mother has shut me in here with my stark-naked cousin. I'm not breathing anymore; I'm invisible; I'm just two eyes behind a towel. Gertrude stands up in the tub, and I can see her whole body; the water runs and drips down curved lines and round forms. She gets the soap and a washcloth and starts to rub it on her, smearing the white foam over her breasts so they move gently in her hands, and her hands move the soapy towel down the stomach, round and round, down the outside of her long thighs, then upward inside her long thighs. She strokes all of her wet body until it's white all over, in streaks and patterns like African body paint. Then she sits down slowly into the steamy hot water and sighs and moans. She lies still in the tub with her chin just touching the water. Two mouthfuls of breast rise up and surface, nipples on top, like two volcanoes, each on its own island. White foam circles the islands like silent surf. She lowers her body a little so that just her lips are above the water and starts to breathe out. The gurgling sound echoes around the tiles, me among them. I have to disappear before she gets out of the tub, have to crawl out the keyhole or something.

Gertrude's face is sweating; she lowers her eyelids, and then her head disappears slowly under, her kneecaps rise, and I notice that she is jerking her head side to side while combing her fingers through her hair. Carefully I stretch my trembling hand from under the towel rail, grab the doorknob, and open the door as quietly as I can. In one swift movement, I'm out in the hallway, closing the door behind me, and as quickly, my heart starts to beat, faster and faster. I'm drenched in sweat, and there's a monstrous pressure in my groin.

Mom walks past the foot of the stairs and sees me standing there, still with my hand on the doorknob. I stare back, but my eyes won't focus.

"Gertrude is taking a bath, dear," she says. "You'll have to wait a bit to go to the bathroom."

I take my hand slowly off the knob, fingers trembling, and speak with a deep, husky voice I've never heard before.

"All right," I say.

"Dinner's ready soon," she says.

"All right."

I float like a whiff of steam into my room, and I'm certain I have a fever now. I'm numb everywhere, even my fingertips. But deep down in my belly, a roaring lava stream whirls. I've never felt like this before, like I'm being fried on a stick, like my head is full of cotton, like my veins are bursting from the pressure of my blood. I lie on my bed and focus on a tiny crack in the ceiling, while my mind starts the replay in slow motion.

I had no idea that breasts could be so beautiful, that a single girl taking a bath had such graceful movements. There must be something terribly wrong with the creation story. How could such beauty be made from a single rib from a normal guy? More likely the guy was made from leftovers when God had finished his true masterpiece: woman. Just like the art teacher used to say when we were supposed to make something from clay: "If there are any leftovers, you can make whatever you want to." That's how it must have been with God; when he had created woman, in all her ethereal beauty, there was a small piece of mud left that was enough for a male.

The door swings open and Gertrude storms through the room in a white bathrobe with a high towel turban on her head, the red towel I had hidden behind. She goes into her room without looking left or right and closes the door, but the warm and sweet fragrance from her body twirls around my room and embraces me. I can't hold back the smile of pleasure that slowly spreads, from somewhere deep down in my belly, across my lips.

Although my cousin is a goddamn brat, intolerable in every sense and the loudest bitch in the Northern Hemisphere, it can't be denied that she's not badly formed by nature. My life would probably be much less interesting if she hadn't forced herself into it, and it's quite possible she even saved it, without having the slightest idea.

Chapter 17

I peek over the edge of *Tintin* and watch my cousin eating her cereal on the other side of the kitchen table. It's 7:25, and Mom is running around the kitchen as usual.

"Here's your lunch box, Josh. Don't be too late, now. Did you finish your homework?"

To avoid answering, I fill my mouth with cereal and make a sound that could be either yes or no.

"There you are—I made some for you too, Trudy, dear," Mom says, and hands my cousin two cheese sandwiches wrapped in aluminum foil. My cousin looks up with disgust.

"You have to eat, you know," Mom says.

"Yes, but not this," my cousin says.

Mom takes her purse out and puts some money on the table.

"Then buy yourself something, dear. You can't go starving, you know." Then she runs for the bus.

Gertrude has her hair down, but one thin strand hangs over her forehead. Her long earring dangles from her ear, and when she leans over the cereal bowl, I can easily watch the curving hills slope down the open neck of her sweater.

Then follows two rope-knitted hills with a deep valley between them.

"What are you staring at?" she shoots out, and looks up, but I disappear behind *Tintin*.

"Nothing."

"You're such an ignoramus." She frowns and stands up. Out in the morning light, rain falls on the kitchen window and I hear the front door slam shut behind her and the sound of her high-heeled boots on the path as she walks toward the bus station. Then all I hear is the ticking clock: 7:45. I still have time to run to school. Five minutes more and I'll be too late, ten minutes and the first lesson will have started. I brood over *Tintin*, reading the text as slowly as I can. Captain Haddock is swearing over some disaster. "Billions of bilious barbecued blue blistering barnacles!" he says. I wonder how many *b*'s there are in this sentence, and I start counting.

The ticking clock slows down until finally I can't hear it anymore. The cereal crackles almost silently in the bowl, raindrops fall on the windowsill outside with gentle plops, someone next door flushes the toilet, the water gushes through the pipes in the wall, a radio is turned on, and I hear the sweeping news melody. It's the eight o'clock news. I'm too late for school.

I run to my bedroom, undress quickly, and crawl under the warm comforter with *Tintin* in my hands. Before I can even read one page, I'm fast asleep.

I wake up extremely well rested but a little confused, and it takes me a long time to stretch fully and look around me. It's like I'm waking up in this room for the very first time. It feels like Sunday. But then I notice my schoolbag in the corner where I threw it yesterday. It's close to noon. My class will be having their lunch; nobody has any idea why I'm not there. Stupid schoolbag. I get a knot of anxiety in my stomach just looking at it. It's like it's staring at me, murmuring, "Truant, truant." I have to get rid of it as soon as possible and everything that's in it. I also have to find a way to get Mom to sign the letter I've written without her knowing what she's signing. If I can manage that, then my liberation will be complete.

It's a strangely comforting feeling wandering around the house in pajamas in broad daylight on a workday. This is what millionaires must do every day. They don't need to work and can just do whatever they want all day. One day I'm going to have so much money that I don't have to do anything. I'm going to have a huge mansion with loads of bedrooms and living rooms and a library. I'll sit in my silk gown, smoking my pipe, having servants bring me chocolate milk and cookies on a silver plate while I read all the books in the world. Mom will have her own part of the mansion all to herself, where she can lie on a big sofa, drink coffee, smoke Kents, and read all the ladies' magazines she likes.

I take my sandwich out of the foil, pour milk over the

chocolate powder in the glass, and stir until the milk turns dark brown. I take a bite of my sandwich and continue to stroll around my future home. Gertrude will be welcome to stay as well. She'll have several rooms of her own. And a gigantic bathroom with mirrors from the ceiling to the floor. But I will have a secret chamber where I can sit and watch her bathe without her noticing me. I follow her in my mind as she walks out of the bathroom into her bedroom. She sits stark naked at her dressing table, combs her hair, and smears body lotion all over her breasts. Then I open the door and walk in, dressed only in my silk robe, with a silk scarf around my neck and a mustache. She looks up and smiles, walks toward me, naked, naked, naked, takes my hand, and leads me temptingly, provocatively toward a huge bed. I lie down, and her face comes closer to mine, her breasts stroking my body until finally they rest on each side of my Adam's apple.

I choke and a bit of bread gets stuck in my throat. I gasp for air and try to cough, try to inhale, but I can't. My throat is blocked. I jump to my feet, stiff with terror. I'm alone in the house. I can't call for help, can't breathe, can't make a sound. I grab my throat and fall to the floor, trying to pat myself on the back. Soaked in cold sweat, I stumble to my feet and throw myself against the door. My feet are trembling, my eyes bulging, my head bursting. Is this how God is going to punish me? Choking me to death on my school lunch because I played truant and spied on my cousin while she was having a bath? My face is boiling. Everything has gone red and black. I'm drooling, dizzy; my feet are cold, my fingers numb. I drop to my knees, double over, and bang my head on the floor. Once. Nothing happens. I strain to lift my head up and let it fall. Twice. I try to raise my head again, but I've lost all sense of direction. Which way is up? Which way is down? My forehead slams to the floor. Third time's the charm? And finally the bread dislodges and shoots from my mouth. A great hissing sound rings in my ears as air rushes into my lungs—breathing in, screaming out, breathing in, screaming out. I stumble to my feet and run to Mom's bedroom. As I rush forward, I stub my toe on the door frame and fall onto the soft comforter, crying out like a toddler. I want to be small again. I want my mom to comfort me, take care of me, dry my tears, stroke my hair, put me to sleep, and protect me from this terrible world. I'm scared and vulnerable, and I want to disappear, to become nothing so no one will remember I ever existed. I want to have never been. I wish for it, I pray to God, I curse God, and I curse the world and school and the injustice of it all. I curse the total lack of understanding, the gym teacher, and finally the government until I'm tired of crying and lie still, sniffling, staring at the doorknob.

It's always dark in here because Mom never draws the curtains—there's no point. It's dark when she wakes up, and it's dark when she comes home. She doesn't draw the curtains until spring. This is her hollow, her shelter from the world, her private corner of the universe. Above her bed is a black-and-white photo of her childhood house, on the bedside table a photo of Granddad, who died when she was a little girl, by the window an easy chair, a knitting basket, and a coffee table loaded with magazines, an old lamp with frills dangling from the lampshade. That's all.

Suddenly I feel unwelcome in here, like I've intruded. This is her sanctuary. I'm no longer a child—she's always saying that—and I shouldn't be here, cuddled up under her comforter. Maybe she's waiting impatiently for me to move out. I have to become an adult soon and put an end to this pathetic nonexistence, become big, bigger, biggest as soon as possible. I dry my nose and stumble out of bed, into the hall—small, smaller, smallest.

I get dressed and shoulder my schoolbag and walk out, avoiding the busy roads and sneaking through yards and alleys instead until I'm down by the steelworks. I run across the street, pass the gas station and behind the fishing sheds, and then I'm out of sight and my wall of rocks appears. I jump from stone to stone until I've reached my rock, and I stand there for a while, watching the blue bay.

Musky gray clouds are slowly torn apart; it's windy, but the air is warm. Everything is gray and wet. The sun is cold, distant and transparent when briefly visible between the passing clouds. I hold the strap of my schoolbag and start to swing it around above my head until it's spinning as fast as a helicopter blade. Then I let go, throwing it out over the ocean, and with it everything that is conscientious, scrupulous, obedient, and submissive. The gulls look over, and for a while they stop fighting at the sewage outlet and follow this unidentified flying object. Then they start the chase, snow-white and greedy. The bag hangs in the air. The strap, which has been weighing heavily on me all my life, sways and waves like an arm trying hopelessly to grab hold of something in thin air, until finally the bag hits the water and floats for a short while. The gulls circle above it, probably hoping it's something edible, but when it sinks, they give up and turn lazily back to the sewage, which is their daily feast.

I'm free. The spell is broken. I am a true man. A man who looks life in the eye and sees it as it is and is not afraid.

When I've made myself comfortable in my little hollow, I take my writing pad out of my pocket, place the point of the pen on the page, and think about Clara. Is she wondering if something has happened to me? I fill up with a tremendous sense of regret. I see her face before me; she tries to be joyful, to hide her sorrow, but it's obvious that she is suffering; the world has been cruel to both of us.

This world would be the darkest place,
Without you here.
And I would be lost in the darkest space,
Without you here.
Here, in my ever hopeful heart. Right here.

You are like the ocean blue,
I am but one drop in you,
No, you're the blooming summer tree,
And I am a leaf on thee.
In my hopeful heart, right here.

Chapter 18

I fold the letter to the headmaster so that the writing is on one side and the other side is blank. I fold a few pieces of paper in the same way and put them all together like a book.

Mom is sewing in the living room and doesn't even look up when I approach her.

"Mom?"

"Hmm?"

"You have to write your signature on these pieces of paper."

"Huh?"

"Your signature. Here and here," I say, and leaf through the pieces of paper.

She looks at me over the brim of her sewing glasses, the machine stops humming, and then she looks at the paper in my hands.

"Why?"

"It's a project in English. Everybody has to bring their parents' handwriting. Then we're supposed to investigate how different people write, or something."

"That's interesting," she says, and smiles. "Where shall I sign?"

"There."

"On each piece?"

"Yes, but just on this side," I say, and hand her a pen.

This is the crucial moment when I could be exposed, but I'm cool as ice; I can't really believe how easy this is. She takes the folded sheets from my hand, places them on the sewing machine, takes the pen, and starts to sign: *Elizabeth Stephenson.*

"A little higher, perhaps," I say. "And farther left."

And she does exactly what I say: *Elizabeth Stephenson, Elizabeth Stephenson, Elizabeth Stephenson,* on every piece.

"There," she says, and hands me the paper, smiling.

"Thanks," I say, and turn and try to walk casually out of the living room. I'm almost there, almost at the door.

"Josh?" she says.

I turn quickly and stare at the wall behind her, because I can't look her in the eye.

"What?"

She looks over the brim of her sewing glasses, staring, reading me like an open book.

"Your pen," she says, and stretches her hand out.

I feel the blood boil in my cheeks as she lays the pen in the palm of my hand. Then she gives me the strangest look.

The sheets of paper fall to the floor.

"What?" I say.

"I was just going to ask if you and your cousin are getting along OK," she says. "Don't you think this will work out fine, at least till spring?"

"Yes," I say, bending down fast, picking up the sheets, making sure the letter is hidden in the middle of the bundle. I stand up again, drying the sweat from my forehead.

"All right, dear," she says, folding the material lying under the needle. "I just wanted to make sure," she adds, and presses the foot pedal. The needle starts hacking away, leaving its zigzag teeth marks in the fabric.

I see her lost in her own thoughts again, all the things she isn't happy about; as long as I'm happy, she doesn't have to worry about me too. And she doesn't. I have a signed letter for my unlimited freedom.

I sit at my desk, reading the letter once over, admiring Mom's signature, in exactly the right place. Then I put the letter in an envelope, lick the glue on the edge, and seal it.

There's whispering outside my window, and a soft cracking sound, like the sound of my cousin's leather jacket. I peek out and notice that somebody has parked a motorcycle by the wall right under my window. This somebody is sitting on the bike, dressed in a leather jacket and jeans, with Gertrude, astride the bike in front of him, and they're eating each other's faces. The boy is holding her butt so tight it looks like he's about to rip it off. I could call Mom, and Gertrude would be sent home immediately; I'd be rid of her once and for all. I could pull the curtains and surprise them by knocking on the window. I'd really like to see that. But then I could just go on watching this spectacle like any other wildlife show on the TV. I can't deny it's quite interesting to watch. Finally they take a break to catch their breath.

"Can't we go inside?" the guy whispers.

"The old bag is home, and the kid as well," Gertrude says.

"Damn. When?"

"Don't know. Soon."

"Kiss me."

"I have to go now."

"Come here, you."

They go for each other's mouths like wolves gobbling up a carcass. Then Gertrude suddenly breaks free from his grip and jumps off the bike.

"That's it, Mike. I have to go now," she says, panting.

"Uh-huh," he says.

She goes to him again, hugs him briefly, gives him a short kiss on the mouth.

"See you tomorrow," she says.

"Uh-huh," he replies.

"Don't start the bike till you're out on the street," she says.

"Uh-huh," he says.

She runs around the corner, and I hear the front door open; Mike fastens his pants and pushes the bike alongside the house and out onto the street, where he starts it with a sudden jerk. The motor roars a couple of times before the bike flies up the street with a high-pitched shriek.

When Gertrude comes in, the noise from the bike is a low hum in the distance. She calls out, "Hello," and goes into the living room to explain to Mom why she's so late. I sneak down the stairs and overhear Gertrude saying she was with a school friend, a girl in her class, studying with her because she has better notes.

"Well, that's nice," Mom says. "But you have to let me know if you don't come straight home from school, just so I know where you are."

"Yes, of course," Gertrude promises.

I hear her come into the hallway, so I jump into the kitchen, whistling innocently so she won't suspect that I know she's been lying. Oh, yes, dear cousin, the ignoramus isn't quite the dimwit you thought he was. Now I really have you under my thumb. You just behave now, or I'll expose you and your lies.

I grin at my image in the window. Then the phone on the table in the hall rings loudly, and my grin freezes. Before the first ring has stopped, I've grabbed the phone off the hook. It's Peter.

"Are you sick?" he asks.

"Yes. It's some kind of a flu," I whisper.

"Who's on the phone?" Mom calls from the living room.

"Just Peter," I say.

"Is it infectious?" he asks.

"Don't know. Think so."

"Is it chicken pox?"

"Why?"

"Mom said that if it was chicken pox, then I should come over. To get infected, you see."

"Why?"

"It's better to have it before you grow up, apparently."

"Nobody knows what this is," I say.

"Did you go to the doctor?"

"I'm having some tests," I say, starting to believe my own lies, feeling dizzy and quite weak.

"Really?" he says.

"Yes," I say.

We say good-bye, and I put the phone down, looking sheepishly around me. But there's nothing to worry about; nobody heard the conversation. The sewing machine hums in the living room, and when I go back up to my room, the music is blaring from Gertrude's room.

The envelope with the letter to the headmaster is lying on my desk, snow-white and clean, innocence itself. Of course, everything in the letter is true; I can't go to school—that's the truth. I neither can nor want to. The only lie is that it wasn't Mom who wrote the letter. But nobody would pay any attention to what I have to say anyway. This is the only way to get some peace, buy me some time to think things over. That's all. Maybe I'll go back to school one day, and then the letter will be long forgotten and Mom will never have to know about it. I haven't lied to anyone, except to Peter on the phone. But he will never find out the truth if I'm careful enough. And then no real harm is done.

Chapter 19

"Where's your schoolbag?" Mom asks, holding a foil-wrapped sandwich in her hand. It takes me a second to think where I put it, when I remember that it's lying at the bottom of the sea.

"It's in my room. I'll take it," I say, and grab the sandwich from her hands.

"Don't forget to put it in your bag, and don't be late," she says while putting on her coat and going.

Gertrude and I are sitting by the kitchen table, and the clock is ticking.

"Aren't you leaving?" I ask.

"Not until half past eight today," she says, yawning over the paper.

If she's leaving late, I'll have to come up with something. But actually I'm not really worried if she discovers my secret; in fact, I can't wait to show her that the fool, her cousin, actually holds her fate in his hands.

"So you have a boyfriend," I say in an indifferent manner, so she doesn't think that I just found out about it. The newspaper lowers slowly, revealing the turnip-white face of my cousin.

"W-Why do you say that?" she stutters, clearly trying to make her voice sound as if this is a ridiculous statement.

"Because I saw," I say.

"Saw what?" she asks in an unbelieving tone but still with the faint shadow of terrible suspicion. She thinks I'm lying. I look straight at her and start to giggle.

"Everything. More or less," I say, and pretend I'm holding the handlebars of a motorcycle, moving my knuckles, making the engine roar. Now she understands that I am no foolish kid. I can be a dangerous enemy if she's going to play tough. She starts to bite the nails on her left hand, stands up, and starts walking in circles, staring at me, her voice the sweetest plea I ever heard.

"Josh, don't tell your mom. Huh?"

I'm covering my face with my hands, giggling. She takes my hands and kneels in front of me, her brown eyes praying for mercy.

"Josh, huh? Please don't."

"Don't what?"

"Tell your mom. She'll kill me. And if my dad hears about this, he'll kill me too. I'll be killed. Understand?"

I shrug and put on the pity-you-but-no-mercy look.

"It's your own fault, isn't it?" I say, and stand up and go into my room. She follows me, her voice breaking into weeping.

"Josh, please, huh? Don't. Please."

She sits on my bed with her hands in her lap. I sprinkle some fish food on the surface of the water in the tank. I didn't imagine this would have such a dramatic impact on her. I thought she'd get mad and would maybe try to beat me up like the other day and maybe try to kiss me again. I'm a little put off, not sure what to say.

"Josh. I'll do anything you ask, anything you want, help you with your homework or whatever, if you just promise not to tell."

"Maybe," I say.

She sits on the bed, weaving her fingers together, uneasy and anxious. I hadn't expected this. I was hoping for a fight.

"I'll think about it," I say.

Then she jumps to her feet and walks right up to me and it's really the first time I realize that she's at least a head taller than me. Maybe she's going to beat me up after all. She puts her hand in her pocket and takes out some money.

"Here," she says, and hands me the money. "You can have all my lunch money if you keep quiet."

I look at the money in her hand. I could do a few things with this much money, buy things. And since I'm an outlaw from society, it'll be good to have some money in my pocket.

"All of it?" I ask.

"All," she says.

I take the money and put it in my pocket.

"But if you tell . . ." she says threateningly, and raises a finger.

"As long as you pay, I won't say," I reply.

And so our mutual trust is secured with mutual suspicion. She gets her schoolbag and says good-bye with a silent look. I'm home alone, free, with my pockets full of money.

Everything downtown is gray; the red houses are red-gray, the yellow ones yellow-gray, the gray ones black-gray. I buy a stamp at the post office with my cap pulled over my face, just in case, so nobody recognizes me. But who would recognize me? Everybody I know is in school. I put the stamp on the envelope and start to put it in the mailbox. I hold it by the slot for a while—I don't know why—but my heart is beating fast. Somebody is standing behind me waiting to get to the mailbox. I slide the envelope inside and hear it fall down gently. Did I definitely put the right letter in the envelope? Was Mom's signature definitely on the letter? I feel a chill. There's no turning back now. I round a corner, heading down to the harbor with my hands in my pockets and my chin to my chest; it feels like all eyes are on me. I walk hurriedly past the shipyard, then the steelworks, and then finally I feel relieved.

The man in the gas-station convenience store tells me the price for a Coke and a chocolate bar as if there is nothing more natural than a boy who should be in school standing here in the middle of the morning, buying a snack. He hands me the change without looking at me.

The shelves on the wall beside him are loaded with

all kinds of things: windshield wipers, fan belts, oil cans, cotton cloths, and tool kits. Then there's one shelf full of plastic toys, and there's a red glider plane with a separate handle and a thick rubber string so it can be shot high in the air. I take it from the shelf and put it on the table. Then the man looks me in the eye. I hand him the money.

"Aren't you supposed to be in school?"

"We have a day off," I say without hesitating.

"And what? Pockets full of money?" he says, watching me suspiciously.

"I'm buying this for my dad," I say, holding the Coke up. "He said I could buy myself something too."

"OK, then," he says, pushing the plane and my change across the counter toward me.

I put everything in my pockets and walk out toward my hollow. I look over my shoulder to check if he's watching me, but he's nowhere to be seen. It is so easy to lie, so terribly easy. And when you've got so much to hide, you can lie so convincingly that you almost start to believe it yourself. Then you give the best performance.

I honestly believe that I'm taking Coke and chocolate to my father, even though there aren't any cargo ships in the docks and Dad is far out at sea. It's just like people who believe in God, even though he doesn't exist. And just like the people who go to church to eat a wafer and sip wine in memory of Jesus, because they believe in him, I sit down in my hollow sipping the Coke and chomping away at the chocolate bar, thinking of my father. He might as well be in heaven; although he is with me, I'm not with him. Half of me is from my father, and so my father is with me. So I wasn't really lying when I told the man I was buying this for my father. This proves that lies can be the honest truth, when you think about it. But my cousin lies to her parents and my mom, just so she can kiss some stupid boy. She's just a sex-crazed female whose sole objective is to find a male to satisfy her burning longings. Probably a close relative to the spider who eats her mate after he's delivered. Is this love, then? To fondle and squeeze and cuddle like a slimy mollusk? Such brutal uncleanliness is certainly the poorest excuse for love there ever was.

Where the rocks end, the sandy beach begins, reaching as far as the eye can see. I run on the beach, for warmth. It's chilly sitting in my hollow drinking Coke. I fasten the wings to my glider, tie the rubber band to the handle, and shoot it into the air. It flies, red and shiny under the blue-gray clouds, and glides high above the beach. I run after it, run from the small waves searching the sand, run and run over seaweed and kelp, run until I see it lower and glide gracefully down, landing next to a gray stone. I pick it up, put the rubber band in the hook on its belly, and shoot it up into the sky again, high and far, higher than the seagulls, higher, higher, until it rests its wings on the mild breeze, flying straight in the air, soaring forward, high above the sand, high above everything.

* * *

I eat lunch in my hollow—the sandwich that Mom made this morning. I'm a free man, looking over the blue bay like a king over his realm. I throw the leftovers to my subjects, the seagulls, who dive down and grab the pieces in the air with a strong flutter of wings, cackling and fighting; that's their lot.

They fight over the bread crumbs till everything is eaten, then they hang around for a while, floating in the air over the rocks in hope of some more, but then they lose interest and fly back to the sewage outlet.

I'm warm after running on the beach, and it's nice to sit in the shelter of my hollow and listen to the lapping of the waves, listen to how they trickle between the rocks. The long-haired seaweed moves lazily to and fro just beneath the surface, and farther out on the bay, a group of eider ducks, *Somateria mollissima,* rises and falls on the undercurrent.

I leaf through my writing pad and read the poems to Clara, each one a sigh from the deepest dungeons of my heart. I think that when I see her in a dream, our souls are meeting. I know it. Even though she laughs with Tommy and makes it look like she thinks he's exciting, I am the one in her heart. It's just so difficult for her to show it. Nobody can understand that better than me.

A loud cackle from a gull tears me from my thoughts. On a rock, not very far away, sits a huge white gull with a black back, *Larus marinus,* looking at me threateningly. He opens his beak and hisses and cackles, loud and clear. He isn't afraid of me in the least and shows no sign of flying away. He is king here, not me. I feel a chilling tingle in my legs; I want to run away but I don't dare to move. He stares at me with one flaming-yellow eye. The coal-black pupil, round like a shirt button, stares without blinking: cold, unscrupulous, merciless. Then he cackles, *He's here! The traitor! The truant! Come and see!*

He fixes this one eye on me and screams, *Away with you! Be gone! To school, to school, to school!*

His wings spread out like two huge swords and beat heavily at the air, flapping and pounding, until I've had enough. I jump to my feet and run. I fall on the rocks, scraping the skin on my hands and knees. I push myself onward, sweating and scared, my heart jumping out of my chest, not looking back, sensing only his yellow beak snapping right at the nape of my neck.

My heart doesn't beat normally again until I'm downtown strolling the streets, jingling the coins in my pocket. I wander into the bookstore. There is a thick scent of paper and pipe tobacco. A man with gray hair sits behind the desk. He's wearing a white shirt and a black vest, and he is talking on the phone when I come in. He notices me, nods in a friendly manner, and continues to talk on the phone. I walk farther into the store, looking at the shelves; there are loads of books here, old books that many hands have touched and caressed, new books that are waiting for someone to open them up and disappear into the world that they hold inside them. Right at the back of the store are shelves of magazines, and there among them is the latest issue of *National Geographic*. Next to it are the women's magazines Mom loves so much, in a long row. On the top shelf are magazines with naked girls on the cover.

I quickly grab *National Geographic* and start leafing through it, pretending to be reading, but my eyes are searching upward, up naked legs, up naked stomachs, up between large breasts. The old guy says good-bye on the phone. Without thinking twice, I reach up, snatch a magazine from the top shelf, and shove it inside my jacket. At the same instant, I hear him put the phone on the hook. I lower my head into the *National Geographic*, put on my most serious natural-scientist face, frown a little, and pretend I'm reading a very interesting article about kangaroos in Australia. I can't see the words for the fog in my eyes; I can't wait to get out, out, out.

"Are you interested in these kinds of magazines?" the man asks, and for a terrible split second I think he means the ones up on the top shelf, but he must be talking about *National Geographic*.

"Yes," I say, but feel instantly that I have to add something, something spicy enough and so convincing that he won't dream of suspecting me of anything, so he won't imagine that I even noticed the magazines on the top shelf.

"My dad is actually a subscriber," I say. "But we have just moved, so the latest issue hasn't arrived yet," I add in a very calm way.

"And you read this?" he asks with the emphasis on *you* like it's a miracle that a thirteen-year-old boy is sufficiently interested in such things to actually read about them.

"Yeah, sure," I say, and force a smile to show him that my interest in natural history goes without saying.

"I'll say," he sighs. "And I thought that old men like myself were the only admirers of that magazine."

But now I feel myself beginning to soar inside, so while I walk casually to the desk, pay for the magazine, watch him take the money, open the register, put the coins in their appropriate compartments, and close it again, I jabber away without a single pause.

"Yeah, you know, I am the president of the Natural History Club at school, and we're actually publishing a magazine very similar, you know. And my friend, well, he's in the club — he's the secretary, actually, and he has this fabulous camera and he's always taking photographs, he even took a photo of a falcon, you know, a real-live falcon. That will be in the magazine, the picture of the falcon, you see, in the first issue that we publish."

"You don't say," the old man says, smiling, when I finish.

My face is very warm and I'm sure I'm all red in the face when I raise my hand and say good-bye and walk out. He nods, holding his pipe between his teeth. There's a mysterious gleam in his eyes; I'm sure he's suppressing a grin. I press the *National Geographic* to my chest, mostly to stop the porn magazine from falling out from under my jacket, and then walk out stiffly like a windup toy. I stumble over the threshold and start to run as fast as I can, convinced that he's found me out and is about to call the police.

When I've gone far enough, I peek around a corner and see him standing outside his store, looking around him with his pipe in his mouth. Then he bends down to pick something up and stands for a while looking at it. It's my red glider. It must have fallen from my pocket when I ran. The old guy looks up and down the street, takes the pipe out of his mouth, and scratches his gray head with the mouthpiece, looks at the glider, shakes his head, and disappears into the store.

What a stupid mistake — my glider lost forever. One thing is certain: I can't be seen in the neighborhood of this store ever again. At least not until I've grown a beard.

I've hardly closed the door behind me when a key turns in the lock and Gertrude appears, chewing gum with a tired look on her face and so feeble she doesn't even bother to say hi. I hurriedly take *Tintin* from my bookcase, slide the magazine from under my jacket, throw it inside the book, and jam it back in the bookcase.

All through supper, Gertrude gives me dark looks, but

I pretend not to notice. She can think what she wants, as long as she pays up. One thing is certain, though: she doesn't trust me. After supper, she offers to do the dishes. It makes Mom really happy, and she sits down at the table lighting a cigarette.

I can't wait for the evening to pass. After I've forced myself to watch the news, I pretend I'm sleepy and go to bed, leaving Mom and Gertrude in the living room. It is obvious that Gertrude is not going to leave me and Mom on our own for a while, just in case.

I hold *Tintin* on the bed in front of me. The magazine nests inside, and I leaf slowly through it with trembling fingers. I feel disgusting but at the same time really cool. This is the worst crime, the lowest place a man can fall: looking at pictures of naked girls.

To begin with, I'm amazed by the somewhat unnatural poses, but at the same time, I'm enchanted by the biological wonder that the female body most certainly is. My cheeks are burning, and I'm dripping sweat in the most unlikely places. I turn the pages, scrutinizing every picture, every spread, gobbling it all up with my eyes. There's a new girl on almost every page, but somehow they all have the same expression: eyes half open, mouths twisted, teeth tight together. Some are on all fours, swaying and twisting with their heads upward and their butts out in the air like cats stretching. It's like they've been electrocuted at the exact moment the picture was taken. The astonishing world of the flesh makes me confused and aroused, limp and tense.

I don't notice Gertrude come into the room until she's standing by the door to her room, looking at me. I look up. My face is a shimmering blaze.

"Still into comics, huh?" she asks.

I nod and pretend to go on reading *Tintin*, but instead my eyes fall right between the legs of Eliza, 22, art student, currently a cocktail waitress.

"Idiot," she says, and disappears into her room.

I turn off the lamp, take my flashlight out of the drawer, slide under the comforter with the magazine, and pull the comforter over my head. Under the comforter the small beam of light creates mysterious shadows; I'm like a Stone Age man in his cave. The girls on the pages seem to come alive in the half-light, crawl out on the sheet, and writhe with pain, stretching their long fingers to the ceiling of the cave, tormented by the burning in their flesh, their sighs and moans echoing in my ears. They're cruel and gentle simultaneously, pulling me closer to them, closer, closer, until I disappear into their restless embraces, completely mad and enchanted, mesmerized and insane, locked up in the Stone-Age man's cave, where all emotions and thoughts are wiped out and only the raw, bloodthirsty instinct of the beast rules, suffocating everything that's tender and beautiful in my consciousness with its ever-burning lava of lust.

I feel a sharp kick in my lower stomach, and a scorching electric wave twists and turns up my spine, blowing my brain into pieces.

For a long time I lie still, sweating and out of breath, in a coma. When I finally come to my senses, I stick my head out from under the comforter. The only thing I hear is the low bubbling sound from the water pump in my fish tank; apart from that, everything is quiet. I jam the magazine under the mattress, turn myself to the wall, and draw my knees up to my chin. The sweat cools down on my skin, and I shudder. I am ashamed. It feels like I'm lying stark naked in the wilderness, utterly alone, despised by everyone. These beauty queens are nothing but delusion and deception. Witches that lay their snares for humans, just to lead them into eternal damnation. I was lured by their sweet promises, but they lured me out into the desert, where nothing awaits me but certain death. And there I die.

Chapter 20

Is man a beast or a civilized being? Can one behave like a beast but still be civilized at the same time? Are we just human beings on the inside but beasts on the outside? Is it beastly behavior to fiddle with oneself, or is it human behavior? I've seen cats and dogs do it, but that's instinct; that's cleanliness. What can it be called, what I've done? It's not cleanliness, but is it instinct? Is it maybe a natural step on the road to becoming a grown-up? But then why do I feel so bad? Why do I feel like a lesser human being? I'm so small I disappear into my bed, blend into the floral pattern on my sheets, feel awkward with every move I make, blush from listening to my own breath. I don't dare to open my eyes because I know I'll suffocate from shyness just seeing my own body, my hands, my fingers, my face in the mirror. I wish something would happen, something terrible and overwhelming, so I could stop thinking about this. If only there were a volcanic eruption or a tsunami. Then nobody would bother speculating why I look so strange. Because what has happened must be written all over my face. I should have jumped into the ocean the other day when I was in the mood. Now I don't dare to get out of bed ever again. I'm just going to lie here, completely still, with my eyes closed, and wait—wait until everything has changed, everything's different, until I'm sixteen or eighteen or something.

From the kitchen, I can hear Mom's and Auntie Carol's voices. It's Saturday morning, and Carol has arrived for a cup of coffee. On Saturdays she delivers *Business Week* to the fancy houses on the west side of town because she claims it's healthy exercise. As it happens, she's a subscriber to *The Socialist Worker* newspaper, because she's left-wing, but maybe delivering *The Socialist Worker* isn't quite as healthy, I don't know, but I've always found it a strange policy to actually be helping the enemy spread his word. But Carol's way of seeing it is probably that this way she's making *Business Week* pay for her subscription to *The Socialist Worker*. It would be just like her to reason like that. She and Mom agree on everything. They agree, for example, that the prime minister is a jerk and that the right-wingers are the same old pains in the asses, out to line the pockets of the rich. They can rant on endlessly about this and about the countless ways the powers that be conspire against them.

Their voices carry up the stairs and into my room, and I pull the comforter down so I can hear what they're talking about properly. They're probably chattering about everything that's wrong with society—criminals in government, criminals in the unions, and criminal employers.

"He can thank his maker that he's still alive," Carol says.

This is the tone of voice she uses when she's talking about my father, and I sit up in bed and listen harder.

"I don't understand what he's doing out on that ship

anyway, with that woman in her condition," she says very clearly.

"Well, it's a good salary, isn't it?" Mom says in a low voice.

"Of course is it," Carol says. "You don't think a woman like that would give up a man like my brother; oh, no, they know how to nail them, first chance they get."

"It takes two," Mom says, even lower than before.

I climb quickly and silently out of bed and creep to the top of the stairs to eavesdrop. Mom offers Carol more coffee, and then there's just the sound of cups hitting saucers.

I've left my weird mood behind me, under the comforter, but my mind is filling up with questions, lining themselves up in a row. Did Suzy nail my father? Nailed him how, exactly? And what takes two? And how does that affect my father's salary?

When I walk into the kitchen, they fall silent as if they're deep in thought and squint at me through the cigarette smoke over the brims of their coffee cups. I get the chocolate for my milk and try to make it look as if I'm completely ignorant of the situation and haven't heard a thing. But they keep looking at me in this strange manner without saying a word.

"What?" I ask.

Then Mom leans toward me and places her hand on my arm and talks in a very soft voice.

"Your father is in the hospital, Josh. It's nothing serious, just a checkup after that accident the other day."

"Goddamn fool," Carol growls, and puts out her cigarette. "Risking his life for some big corporation. And the only thing they do is send him for some stupid checkup so they don't get sued by the insurance company."

"He'll be in overnight," Mom says, and strokes the back of my hand.

"Well, so he says," Carol adds. "You see, there grows a lovely flower out in the country," she says, giggling, and lights another cigarette.

"Maybe you'd like to visit him," Mom says, and I can tell she doesn't like the way Carol is talking, but as usual, though she's offended, she doesn't say anything. But I sense exactly how she feels, and suddenly I want to embrace her because now I feel like her. And I want to ask her forgiveness for how wicked and deceitful I've been. But I say nothing and I don't move but fill up with grief and regret and loneliness until my face swells from the bottled-up emotions, which I keep down by clamping my lips tight, just like my mom does. If only Carol wasn't here, then I would have let go.

"Can I go today?" I ask.

Mom gives Carol a questioning look, as if she controls the visiting hours at the hospital, like she's in charge of everything and Mom nothing. As if Mom can't decide if I can go and visit my own dad at the hospital.

"Wait till tomorrow," Carol says. "Then we'll see if he's still there."

"Maybe you'd like to go and play with Peter," Mom

says, and suddenly I realize she wants me to go away so she and Carol can keep on talking about this thing that's obviously none of my business. I slurp my chocolate milk and instantly couldn't care less about how Mom feels. And I don't want to beg her forgiveness anymore, don't feel I've been bad or deceitful at all; I'm just me, and it's none of her business what I do with my life.

"Maybe," I say, and walk out of the kitchen.

As usual, Carol makes a comment, which she doesn't mean me to hear, but I hear it anyway.

"How moody he's becoming!"

I want to turn around and scream at the bitch, but my mother's genes grab at my throat, so I turn blue in the face instead of uttering the slightest word.

Moody in Carol's language means being an idiot or retarded or both simultaneously. If only she could hear the insults and swearing piling up in my throat. I put my clothes on and feel even smaller than when I woke up; I'm shrinking continuously, and soon I'll disappear for good. No, I'm not going to Peter's. I want to be on my own today, completely alone. Still, I'm not brave enough to go to my hollow; the seagull might have taken it over, the rotten beast. Ambushing me and screaming at me and scaring me to death. I'm going to the hospital to visit my father. If he's asleep, then I'll sit by his side until he wakes up, and nobody can pull me away from him.

Gertrude opens her door and peeks out.

"Can I talk with you?"

She hardly has anything on, but when I enter her room, she's wrapped a bathrobe around her.

"What?"

"Will you do me a favor?"

"Like what?"

"Mike has invited me to a party tonight."

"So? Why should I care?"

"Could you tell your mom that I'm at a school dance and might be late because after the dance I'm visiting my girlfriend who's babysitting?"

"What girlfriend?"

"There is no girlfriend, of course."

"Oh?"

"I'm just asking you to tell your mother there is one."

"Why don't you do it yourself?"

"Because she'll see right away that I'm lying. And I don't want to lie to her, either."

"But you think it's all right for me to lie to her?"

Gertrude reaches into the pocket of her bathrobe and hands me a bill. I look at it in her hand, or rather, I'm making it look like I'm looking at the bill. In reality I'm looking at her bare chest where her robe has opened slightly. She has a very thin gold chain around her neck and a tiny birthmark just a little lower, right where her breasts begin to fill up her skin.

"Will you do it or not?"

I pretend I have to think about this. I dig my fists deep

in my pockets, sit on her bed, and try to make it seem as if I'm looking right past her, but I'm gobbling her up with my eyes. Her scent twirls up from her sheets, and I could sit here all day long just breathing in. Most of all, I want to lie down in her bed and drown my face in her pillow.

"Answer me," she says. "Yes or no?"

"All right, then," I murmur, and put my hand out.

She reaches forward and places the bill in my palm, but at the same time the robe slides off her thigh so I can almost see all the way right up to her groin.

"I have to get dressed," she says.

"You want me to tell her now?" I ask, just to prolong my stay a bit.

"Of course not. Not until tonight after I've left."

"Dad's in the hospital," I say, and suddenly I want to ask her to come with me to the hospital to visit him. I wish she were my big sister; then I wouldn't have to ask her.

"What happened?"

I tell her about the checkup because of the accident on the ship and I try to talk slowly. It's so nice to sit here in her room, I want to stay longer, want to sit and chat with her about something, anything, and breathe in her scent. But she's impatient, has no time to listen, is in no mood to talk to me, and cuts me off.

"And what in God's name was he thinking, risking his life, expecting a baby and all?" she says.

My narrative fades out to stutter and mumble and my jaw drops a little.

"Huh?"

"You didn't know?"

"Uh, no. Yes, I did," I add quickly so she doesn't think I'm a complete idiot.

"Well, that's how it is," she says, crossing her arms over her breasts and giving me a firm look.

I haul myself out and traipse along into my own room and sit on my own bed. This is all too much for me. Too many things happening at the same time, as if the world is falling apart all around me and there's nothing I can do to prevent it. Why doesn't anybody tell me anything?

So I'm getting a half sibling, a little brother or a little sister out in the countryside. Where the hills go on for so many miles that it takes days to walk across them, where the lake is so deep you could never reach the bottom, where the summer is so warm that you can run in your shorts all day long, where the scent of nature is so strong you can taste it. All this my father would tell me years ago and always with the promise that we would go there next summer. Next summer. But we never went there, and now he's gone and found a woman there and they are expecting a baby.

Carol has left seven Camel stubs with pink lipstick in the ashtray. I sit at the kitchen table, watching Mom as she puts potatoes in the pot.

"Is Trudy awake?" she asks, and looks out the kitchen window at something in the far distance.

"Yes," I say.

"Lunch will be ready soon," she says.

Her blank face reflects in the glass; there's a low screeching from the latch on the open window; the wind is blowing harder.

We stay like this for a long time without saying anything, just listening to the water boil in the potato pot; the steam pushes the lid gently so it tingles lightly by the brim of the pot and the boiling water rumbles in a deep voice underneath, but now and then a single drop falls with a sharp hiss on the hot stove.

Chapter 21

There's a thick stench of medicines and cleaning products in the elevator; the walls are steel, but the floor is pale-green linoleum. I step out on the fifth floor and walk along a hallway, peeking into the rooms. He wasn't on the fourth floor or the third; at least I didn't see him there. I don't dare to ask the nurses because I'm not sure about the visiting hours; maybe they'll tell me to go away and come back later. I'll just have to find him myself, and I will look in every room, on every floor, until I do.

There are a lot of old people in these beds. They're sleeping on the snow-white pillows in snow-white shirts under snow-white sheets in snow-white rooms. They're like newborn babies in cradles, their hair ruffled, their faces wrinkled, eyes closed but mouths open; their souls far, far away somewhere in a peaceful dream. But some of them wince, and then one shouts and it echoes down the hallway. A nurse is pushing a cart in front of her, but two others go into the room where the shouts are coming from. I try to stay invisible, but the nurse stops the cart right in front of me.

"Are you looking for somebody?"

"Yes."

"Grandmother or grandfather?" she asks, smiling.

"Dad."

"And he's supposed to be here?"

"I think so."

"What's his name, dear?"

"Oliver."

"And last name?"

"Stephenson."

"He's not on this floor," she says, looking at me with suspicion, as if I'm wandering here on false pretenses.

"What's he here for?"

"A checkup, I think."

"What was the matter with him?"

"There was this accident on board the ship he works on, the *Orca*?"

"Oh, yes, I know. Are you his son?" she says in a gentle tone, suddenly becoming very concerned, all suspicion gone. She asks me to wait and walks to a glass cage, where she talks with three nurses, who turn their heads simultaneously, looking in my direction and talking all at once. One of them picks up a phone, but the others look at me through the glass. When the phone conversation is over, they whisper something among themselves and the one who was talking on the phone comes out into the hallway. She has a watch hanging on the left side of her chest and a name tag that says Brenda.

"Hello, dear," she says, and sits beside me on the bench. "My name is Brenda. What is your name?"

"Joshua."

"Well, now, Joshua. There has been some kind of misunderstanding, about your dad, I mean."

I look at her, and I don't understand what she's talking about. There's a contraction in my throat.

"He left this morning. He was fine, so we didn't need to keep him. He was hurrying home—long trip back to the countryside, he said. Didn't he call your mom? Didn't you know he was on his way home?" she asks, placing a gentle hand on my shoulder.

But I can't answer. Everything's stuck, and my eyes are burning. There aren't any simple answers to those questions. She thinks we're all a happy little family, dad, mom, boy, and beautiful countryside. She thinks Mom and I have come all this way to fetch an injured dad, to take him home and care for him. This woman doesn't know anything.

I stare at the pale-green linoleum that smells of floor wax, and my throat is aching. I purse my lips and try to swallow. Usually that works fine. But now it's not working quite as well. Maybe it's the smell of the floor wax; maybe it's this woman sitting beside me, smelling so clean and a little of perfume, with her thick, warm hand on my shoulder. And the harder I purse my lips and the more I try to swallow, the worse the aching in my throat and the pain in my eyes is. It reaches far into my head. Then I feel the strong and warm hands embrace me, and I fall into her sweet-scented bosom, and the watch hanging on her chest is right by my ear, ticking almost in rhythm with my heart.

I wish she was my mom and would carry me into a snow-white room, undress me, lay me in a snow-white bed, cover me with a snow-white sheet, and sit by my side until I fall asleep like the old people, like the little babies, so I could dissolve somewhere far way into a peaceful dream, maybe to the end of the world, where the summer is so warm that you can run in your shorts all day long, where the scent of nature is so strong you can taste it.

I don't know why she is so especially kind to me. Maybe she is like that with everybody who comes here and doesn't find who they're looking for.

I sniff vigorously and dry my nose carefully on my jacket sleeve.

"Where's your mom?" she asks.

I can't answer right away because my nose is clogged and the linoleum is just a haze before my eyes.

"Home," I say.

"And where is 'home,' dear?" she asks in the same gentle tone as if she's doing wordplay with a little boy who's just begun to talk. She reaches into her pocket and hands me a tissue.

"Can I call someone to pick you up?" she asks.

"No," I say, and blow my nose.

"Are you sure, dear? Shouldn't I call your mom?"

"There's no need," I say, and try to think of something to say so she doesn't call anyone.

"I'll just go to my auntie's," I say. "She lives close by."

I rise slowly from her soft chest, hanging my head. I can't look up, am paralyzed with shyness and shame.

"I'm awfully sorry," she says, and strokes my cheek.

"It's all right," I say, and stand up but can't look up and don't know what to do or say, but I want to thank her for being so kind to me, so I put out my hand.

"Thanks."

But she doesn't take my hand. Instead she holds out her arms and embraces me warmly. Then she leads me to the elevator. She pushes the lobby button for me, and just before the door shuts, I can finally look up and watch her where she stands, raising her hand like she's saying farewell to somebody she cares about: blond hair, dressed in white, like an angel.

I walk past the cemetery overlooking the sea, and it's not until I reach the point where you can get onto the shore that I stop whimpering and sit on a rock and look out over the ocean. It's windy, and the waves are green with white crests. The clouds sail fast overhead, and the sun, distant and cold, glimmers occasionally on the waves, flickering on the pebbles on the shore, on a blue shell by my feet, half buried in the sand.

"'March: the sun is rising slow, but surely it will win,'" I mumble to myself and dig my toes into the sand.

He's gone to the country. His girlfriend is sitting by

his side, and they're kissing. He's stroking her belly, where their child is growing, the child that will be my sister or my brother. And I don't even know if we'll ever even meet or get to know each other. When this child is thirteen, I'll be twenty-six, maybe married with a family, maybe living in another country. Maybe dead.

The waves rise and fall out on the bay like a silent echo of each other until they melt into the sand on the shore with a low whisper: *Maybe, maybe, maybe.*

Mom comes into the living room with cookies on a plate and a mix of orange juice and lemonade in a jug. There's a movie starting on TV. I lie on the floor, sipping the frothy mix and munching the sweet cookies. It's been a long time since Mom and I have watched TV together. I haven't quite brought myself to tell her what Gertrude paid me to lie about. But then she's the one who forces me to do it by asking me.

"What's happened to Trudy?"

"There's a school dance, I think."

"Really?"

"Yeah, then she's going to her girlfriend's after the dance. She's babysitting or something."

"When did she tell you this?"

"I met her outside, today, I think, I mean, I don't remember. But she asked me to tell you."

"She didn't say a word to me," Mom says, and sits in her chair.

This will be the last time I lie for my cousin, no matter how much she pays me for it. Out of the corner of my eye, I notice the look on Mom's face; she's worried and suspicious. But she asks no further.

"Is this a good movie?" I say to make an effort to lure back the comfortable atmosphere that was in the living room just a moment ago. But Mom has her mind elsewhere.

"Are you going to visit your father tomorrow?"

"No," I reply.

"He would be happy to see you."

"Peter and I are going to do stuff tomorrow."

"Are you sure?"

"The film is starting," I say, and turn up the television.

It's the film about the bell ringer in Notre-Dame Cathedral in Paris. Quasimodo: the horrible hunchback, who is really very kind, but everybody is afraid of him and mocks him because he's ugly and deformed. But he loves this one girl, Esmeralda, who has long black hair, almond eyes, and beautiful lips like Clara. When the mob has taken Quasimodo and tied him to the platform in the middle of the square, they shout at him and throw trash and rotten vegetables at him. He's utterly helpless, tied up on his hands and knees. He asks for water. He shouts and cries, "Water, water," but the mob laughs. Then, she alone steps from the screaming mob, Esmeralda, like an angel from heaven, with water in a jug. She's not afraid of him; she doesn't despise him. She steps onto the platform and gives him water, and everybody stares in silence at the merciful act. I don't see Quasimodo and Esmeralda anymore, only Clara and myself; the hunchback inside me yearns for the water that only she can give me.

Chapter 22

During the day, my mind is full of dreams of my heavenly Esmeralda, but during the night the witches appear and work over me in feverish fantasies and I go to them with disgust and longing at the same time. They dance like mad devils under my comforter right before my eyes until everything is over and I fall asleep in guilt and shame, my heart feeling like a black stone. Am I going crazy, or are girls really so double sided? Were those devil women once like Clara, innocent and pure? Maybe they aren't even human; maybe they're kept in cages in the offices of those magazines and let out once a month for a photo session. Is this love? This burning pressure in the pit of my stomach during the night? Or is love the bittersweet mournful bliss that I feel during the day? Which emotion is the true one, the one that burns or the other that warms?

My mind is a circus in flames where all the animals have broken out of their cages, kicking, jumping, screaming, and fighting in desperation to get out before the burning tent falls over them. I'm exhausted, and I don't know what is right or wrong anymore, lie or truth. I want, so much, to talk to someone about all this, but I don't know who that could be.

If I only could talk to God, man to man, then he could set me free with one word. But the only solution the Holy Book has to offer is "Go and sin no more." That's easier said than done. And what is sin? Is it a sin to be a human being, to hurt, to find no answers, only more questions? Or is it a sin to be a beast that wants so much to become a human being?

Mom has gone to church, and she didn't even try to make me go with her. Maybe she's noticed that it isn't working. Maybe she's given up on me. Maybe she thinks I can stand on my own two feet in front of God now that she's given me the Bible. But maybe she just doesn't care what happens to me anymore and can't be bothered to try to save me by dragging me along to church. Maybe she thinks I'm lost already. Yes, I'm like the prodigal son who demanded his inheritance in advance and spent it all in debauchery and extravagance. And I'm a liar and a truant and a sinner on top of that. I can't bear to think ahead to when my secrets are discovered; I must use the time well to find some answers, to understand my life, figure out what to do. But it doesn't matter how much I think—I can't find any answers, only more questions. Maybe I really am going mad. How could any sane person think of doing what I've done? Maybe that's why Mom has gone to church alone. She's figured out that I'm out of my mind, and she's praying to God for strength to send me to an asylum. Then the doorbell rings, and I'm convinced that on the staircase are two massive police officers along with a group of male nurses in white with a straitjacket ready.

But it's only Peter.

"Reporting for duty, sir!" he says with the harsh soldier's grimace on his face, snapping his hand to his forehead and his heels together so it echoes in the hall.

He can be so childish. I don't move a muscle, just nod. When his salute isn't answered, his hand moves down; he smiles apologetically and probably thinks he dragged me out of bed with a deadly fever.

"Mom wanted me to visit you," he says.

"Oh?"

"To get infected," he says.

"Really?"

He follows me up to my room and sits by the desk, but I sit on the bed and don't know what to say to him. I don't feel like talking to him now; I have nothing to say.

"Can you breathe in my face?" he says.

"Huh?"

"Breathe in my face," he repeats, and lets out a breath to show me what he means.

"Why?"

"To infect me."

I place myself in front of him, and he closes his eyes and opens his mouth and I take a deep breath and blow into his mouth, and he inhales at the same time.

"One more time," he says. "Just to be certain."

After I've repeated the procedure, I move back to sit on the bed and try to look sick, but Peter stands up and looks into the fish tank.

"How's school?" I ask, to make him think that I'm devastated about missing it.

"You know," he says, and shrugs.

"No one else sick?" I ask.

"No," he says. "Now you have time to write about the falcon for our magazine."

"I feel dizzy if I write," I say.

Peter sits back in the chair, spins in a circle, and then leans forward, his face beaming with exciting news.

"Ari beat up Tommy!" he says.

He gloats while he describes what happened.

"There was a fire drill on Friday," Peter says, and immediately I regret that I wasn't there. Everybody knows that fire drills at our school are the best. Because the school building is so old, the fire brigade itself has to come for our drills to put up this huge slippery cloth from the balcony all the way down to the playground. Then everyone has to slide down it really fast, under their watchful eyes, to the great applause of everyone already in the playground, watching and clapping.

"And when it was Miss Wilson's turn, her skirt flew right up her legs! She couldn't decide whether to cover her eyes or hold her skirt down!" Peter says, laughing, and I can just picture Pinko coming right after her, rigid like a general as usual, self-assured and serious with his red tie flying up in his face.

"Our class was the last one, and the girls had to go first, according to the rule: women and children first. Finally everybody was down except Tommy and Ari.

"But then Tommy pushed Ari to the side because he wanted to throw himself down," says Peter. "But Ari grabbed Tommy's collar and dangled him in thin air, like a kitten, and then gave him a good one on the nose, before throwing him headfirst down the cloth! Then Ari jumped after him, flying like a cannonball driving his heels full force into Tommy's ass," says Peter, laughing.

"I can just picture Tommy dangling in Ari's grip," I say, and laugh out loud. I can't believe I missed this; why does school suddenly become fun the one day I decide to play hooky?

"You just left after gym the other day?" Peter asks, and then I stop laughing.

"Yeah. Suddenly I just felt really sick," I say.

"Sandra said you screamed at her."

"Shower Sandra?"

"Yes."

"That was just because I felt so horrible," I say as sweat begins to sprout on my forehead, and to avoid suspicion, I lie on the bed and moan a bit and hold my head.

"I can't laugh too much," I explain. "It gives me a headache."

But I'm thinking how Mr. Penapple must be proud of his son and how Ari is lucky to have a dad who works on dry land and wants him to help in the fish shop. It's easy to be brave when you have a father. Then, no matter what happens, everything will turn out all right.

Peter turns the falcon on the desk and investigates every feather. He's saying something I don't hear, because my mind has turned into a screaming circus elephant running wild again. Before I realize it, I've blurted out the things that are on my mind.

"Why don't they teach us about anything that matters in school?"

"What do you mean?" Peter asks.

"Just, you know. Things that matter."

"Like what?"

"I don't know. Just something about life," I say, and am already regretting having opened my mouth in the first place.

"We do math and literature," says Peter.

"I know."

"And PE and geography and history," he counts on his fingers.

"I know that," I say.

"And physics and French and English and biology and about Christianity," he adds. "What more do you want to learn?"

"I don't know," I say, and sit up in bed. "But you're never going to need any of that, or most of it," I add.

175

"You need to know how to read and write and do math," he says, and he sounds as if he's a bit shocked.

"I just want to learn something else as well."

"Like what?" he asks, irritated. "There is nothing else. Not until you get to college."

"For example, to think," I say, but feel at once that I'm on thin ice.

Peter shakes his head, turns on the chair, crosses his arms over his chest, and snorts. "That can't be taught," he says. "I mean, everybody thinks; it's innate."

"What do you think about?" I ask.

He sighs and looks around him like he's searching for an answer, turns the chair, making the wheels squeak, scratches his head, and picks his nose.

"I think about school, about my homework. I think about what I'm reading when I'm reading. I think about what I'm saying when I'm talking. I think about what I'm watching when I'm watching something, what I hear when I'm listening to something, and sometimes I don't think at all."

"But don't you ever feel that you are different from who you are, I mean that you're not really who everybody thinks you are?"

"I'm just me," he says, astonished. "I can't be anybody else. What kind of flu do you really have?" he asks. Maybe he's regretting having come over to be infected.

"I guess there's something wrong with my brain." I sigh.

We're silent for a while, and the only noise is the bubbling of the water pump in the fish tank and the squeaking of the chair as Peter turns it from side to side. I shouldn't have started talking about this. Now he definitely thinks I'm crazy, which is probably true, but it would have been better to keep it secret.

"There's going to be a costume party at school soon," he says.

"Oh, really?" I say, with great interest to cover up how bad I feel, relieved that he says something so both of us can forget that stupid conversation.

"I was thinking of going as a gorilla," he says.

"Really," I say. "Cool."

Then we don't say anything, but Peter turns on the chair and whistles a tune. I sit up in bed and wait for him to leave. But then he starts telling me about a movie he saw with his dad yesterday, and I pretend to listen.

I feel like there's so much distance between Peter and me. Once we were so close, but not anymore. When I watch him speak now, he seems so childish, so naive. I never thought I would feel that way about Peter. I thought he was the coolest guy; I worshipped him, found everything he did or said brilliant, everything his father did, everything his mom said. What's changed? While this question runs through the flames in the circus in my head, I hear a voice, almost like my own. It resounds in my head like it's coming through a huge sound system: *It's you, Josh Stephenson. You've changed.*

I sit stupefied on the bed, watching Peter's lips move, but I can't hear a word he's saying. It's like this voice has calmed the frenzy in my mind, put out the fire, comforted the animals, and led them back to their cages. And suddenly I realize I'm perfectly at ease.

"Are you listening?" I suddenly hear Peter say as if the volume of his voice has been turned up.

"Yeah," I say, and go on pretending to listen.

Finally, when Peter has told me the entire story line of the movie, and repeated it, because he forgot a part that happened in between, and I haven't done anything except nod my head, he starts to describe the ending, which is so complicated and manifold that it takes him longer to tell me about the last ten minutes than the whole movie. When he stands up to leave, I don't have to pretend to be feeling feeble. When he's gone, I lie on my bed, glad to be home alone on a Sunday and grateful for the silence in my head.

Chapter 23

It almost feels like spring when I walk down to the harbor and there's nobody around; the day is bright and still, almost no wind. Sundays are days of tranquillity, of rest, and for the first time in a long while, my mind is not spinning around but calm and smooth like the sea below my hollow.

I start to listen to the soft breeze, listen to the whispering lapping under the rocks, listen to myself breathe. And then it's like I'm hearing that voice inside my head again.

"There you are," it says, and it sounds almost like my own.

And I think I can see him out of the corner of my eye, the boy that this voice belongs to. He could be wearing a blue cap, pulled down low, a brown raincoat, jeans, and sneakers, like me.

"Who are you?" I ask, though I don't need to ask, because I think I know the answer. But I ask anyway because I want to hear him talk.

The stillness is so thick I can feel it resting in the palm of my hand, touching the tips of my fingers, and the scent of seaweed is salty and fresh.

Maybe he's standing there, by the red rock, looking around him with a smile on his lips like he's remembering the good days when he came down here with a catapult to shoot at the seagulls or throw a line and tackle out from the rocks, far out to sea, and sat in the shelter of the hollow when the spring rain trickled down and the fish nibbled the hook.

"You know very well who I am," he says, and sends me a teasing smile.

"Maybe you're just a genie from a bottle," I say, but then he laughs and I do too.

His hair pokes out from under his cap and his eyes are like mine, but his face is brighter and happier. He picks up a pebble and throws it far out onto the calm water. The stone disappears with a low clap and ignites circle after circle on the smooth surface. He sits on the red rock and watches the circles grow wider and stretch out until they subside and disappear and the ocean gleams, untouched.

He is the boy who fell asleep the night before my thirteenth birthday, but I am the one who woke up the day after. I'm the one who sweats and gets chills when I look at Clara, not him. I'm the one whose voice is breaking and who's getting pubic hair, not him. I'm the truant. I'm the deviant. Not him. He is twelve years and 364 days old. I'm merely a newborn.

He's the one who learned to walk and talk, read and write and do math, the little he can. He learned to think and imagine and conclude and understand. He became a perfect intelligent human being. And as soon as he reached that point, he had to step aside because I was born.

"You're so serious," he says into the silence. He takes off

his cap and ruffles his hair, the same way I sometimes do when my head's hot.

"I'm just thinking," I say, and look at some eiders rocking gently on the undercurrent.

"Remember how much fun it was to fish here?" he asks.

"Yes," I say.

"Why have you stopped doing that?"

"Well, you know, what's the point?"

He shrugs and draws down the corners of his mouth, but then he looks at me sideways, squints, and grins.

"It's the teenage thing, isn't it?" he asks.

"I guess so," I say.

"What a state to get yourself into," he says. "Look at Gertrude. Do you think her behavior is normal?"

"No, not at all."

"Far from it," he says. "But I guess it's something everyone has to go through, in their own way."

I wonder if Clara is going through this too, I think.

"Of course," he says. "I guess it's pretty much like waking up in a cradle one day, not being able to talk or walk."

"Do you think you know everything?" I say, slightly irritated by how cocky he is.

"I'm a perfect intellectual human being," he says. "You said so yourself just now."

"I only thought that."

"Well, I heard it anyway," he says, and throws another pebble far out to sea. The pebble hits the surface and skips once, twice, three times.

"Did you see that?" he says joyfully, watching the circles on the surface grow wider.

"Why haven't we talked before?" I ask.

"You have been so preoccupied with yourself, whining in your hollow, day after day, writing poetry! And when you were thinking of killing yourself! I thought you had gone mad. Tell me, how in the world could you sit there for a whole day, making up obituaries about yourself?"

"You don't know what it's like," I say to silence him.

"No, that's true," he says. "But I can sort of imagine."

"Can you imagine anything about me and Clara?" I ask suddenly.

"That's your problem."

"Didn't you claim to have answers to everything?" I ask.

"If I had all the answers you needed, then your existence would be perfectly without purpose. You have to find your own answers."

He stands up like he wants to leave. But I don't want him to leave; I don't want to lose him. He runs his fingers through his hair, and I suddenly feel such a strong emotion, such affection. And I no longer care if he thinks he's wiser than he is, because I used to be him. Everything he tried has made me who I am now; everything he sowed, I have reaped. How could I forget that he used to be me?

"People often forget who they used to be," he says, and puts his cap on.

The breeze has become colder, and he puts his hands in his pockets.

"If you forget yourself, though, you could lose yourself and then there's nothing left," he adds.

"Nothing?"

"Well, flesh and bones and a heart that beats and a brain that thinks and hands and feet that move and a mouth that speaks. But the real you is not there anymore."

"Where will I be, then?"

"How should I know?" he says. "You'd probably be where you lost yourself."

"Can't you stay with me?" I ask. "And help me through all this?"

"I can't hold your hand all through your teens, Josh. These are the years you have to learn to handle life. And yourself," he says, and sits back on the red rock. "I mean, who did I have when I was growing and changing? Nobody! Unless you count God Almighty, perhaps."

He leans forward, resting his elbows on his knees.

"If you just think of me once in a while, think back to the time when you were me and remember how you felt, how you always found answers to every question, how everything you did was almost perfect, then maybe it won't be so bad. It will be difficult, but not hopeless."

"But what happens when I've learned to handle life and myself? What happens then?"

"I don't know," he says thoughtfully. "Maybe then another Josh will appear, the one that takes over from you. Maybe human beings never go past twelve years old; maybe every year you live is like a month in a usual year. Then when the year ends, it never comes back, except in memory. But at the same time, a new year begins and a new life. And the Josh that comes after you has to learn his lessons, ask his own questions, and find his own answers. Maybe this human existence is something like that."

"Maybe," I say, deep in thought.

"Yes, maybe," he says, and we look for a long time out over the water where the eiders rise and sink on the undercurrent in a gentle rhythm like a single soul in many bodies.

It's become dark. The lights on the island across the bay glitter in the distance, and the beam from the lighthouse cuts through the darkness with a lazy pulse. I've made a little fire in front of my hollow because I want to sit here a little longer. A moment ago, I thought he was gone. Then I stood up and gathered some pieces of wood and made a small pile. But when I sat by the fire and looked into the flames, it felt like he was still sitting on the red rock over there. Out of the corner of my eye, I saw a handful of warm light fall on his face.

"Do you think Jesus really existed?" I ask without taking my eyes off the flames.

"I guess so," he says.

"But do you think he really did perform all those miracles that are in the Bible?"

"Maybe," he says.

"But, I mean, how did he walk on water, huh? It's impossible."

"Anybody can do that," he says, like there's nothing to it.

"Not me."

"Sure you can," he says. "If you think a little, then you understand you can."

I think for a long while, rack my brain, and try to come up with all kinds of methods, but I'm no closer to a solution.

"Think harder."

"Did he use a float?" I ask hesitantly.

"Of course not."

"I don't know how he did it, then," I say. "Are you telling me that you've walked on water?"

"Yes."

"Oh, yeah? When?"

"Do you have any idea how much effort it is to learn to walk on your own two feet and keep balance?"

"No."

"Well, that was my miracle," he says. "And to learn to talk and read. And not least to think. Don't you understand? Walking on water is conquering what seems impossible. Turning water into wine is changing what you have into something better."

"But these were miracles. I can't do any miracles."

"It's up to you. Have it your way. But if you're going to mature at all, you'd better start doing some miracles on yourself."

"But I don't believe in Jesus. He's either a lamb or a shepherd, a god or a man. And I'm bored in church."

"You don't have to believe in anything if you don't want to. But if you're going to walk on water, you have to believe in yourself at least. Or else you sink."

There's a thin mist over the bay now, and the lights on the island have disappeared. Everything is dark and black, the rocks around me, the sky above me, the sea below me. And it's cold. Only the small fire warms my face and hands and throws a red glow on the rocks. The embers light up and fade in the wood with a low crackle. Tiny tongues of flame lick the gray wood until they turn black, shrink, and break and crumble down between the rocks.

"Mom believes in the Bible and God and all that," I say.

"That's her choice, the thing she clings to," he says. "But it doesn't matter. You can believe in one thing today and something else tomorrow, but it has nothing to do with life. The only thing that matters is knowing what you're going to do, and then doing it."

The flames lower and the light subsides until the tongues of fire become as small as candle flames. Finally, only the embers are left in the black darkness.

The sea is lapping under the rocks, and the undercurrent has become heavier. The black water gleams as a wave rises and then falls with a tired sigh on the rocks, trickling under them and in between them. It takes a long time to trickle away, thick and slow like tar, and when the ocean has dragged it back, it's like it hesitates for a while, holding its breath for a moment, before it breathes the wave out again, slowly, sleepily, and the wave falls in, embracing the rocks below me.

"I miss Dad," he says in a low voice.

Then I feel how lonely he is and scared, despite his courage and wisdom, and I want to embrace him, encourage him, and show him that whatever happens, he'll always have me. I wish I could take him in my arms and be his friend and comforter. But he's gone, and there's nobody here by the burned-out embers except me.

Chapter 24

I'm a twinkling star, far away in space, on a billion-light-year search for another star so the two of us can twinkle together, side by side, rotating around each other. But stars only *seem* to be close to each other; in fact, there's a vast, unbridgeable gap between them. They travel at different speeds in different directions, and each one is on its own path. I will never ever get close enough to any of them so I can twinkle with it for a while. That happens very seldom, maybe only every million years or so.

I wake up to the tinkling of bracelets and whispering in the hall, and at once I realize that the starry space is just the darkness behind my eyelids and I watch my star twinkle and sparkle and grow smaller and smaller until it disappears. There's a noisy crackle of leather on the other side of my door and a strange smell that seeps in by the door frame; a strong smell of gasoline and sweat. Then the blood-red face of Gertrude appears in the doorway.

"I need to ask you a favor," she says, and her slithering body twitches in the doorway. "Can you stand guard for us and let us know when your mom comes home?"

"Us?" I ask at the same moment that marvelous Mike appears behind her with a wolfish grin under his long hair.

"What are you going to do?" I ask, although such a question is a bit stupid.

"Oh, please," Gertrude says, irritated, and points Mike to go into her room.

He drags himself over the floor, points a finger at the falcon, and says, "Cool," and then swings with rubber legs into her room, and a loud creaking is heard as he throws himself on her bed.

"This is the least you can do for me," Gertrude says, and the bracelets tinkle with impatience.

"Am I supposed to stay awake all night while you two are . . . ?"

"Haven't I done lots of things for you?" she hisses in my face. "I've given you money and everything. God, you're petty."

She could beat me up, but that wouldn't change any-thing, I'm not going to sit here like an idiot while they're going at it next door. Gertrude can do whatever she wants; that's her responsibility and I'm not going to have any part in it.

"You can stand guard yourself. Maybe you could even take turns," I say, and grin, because that's obviously not what they intend to be doing. I stand up from my bed and sit triumphantly at my desk. The falcon stands erect by my side, and both of us look, gloating, at my poor cousin, who doesn't know what to do. But then she suddenly bends down toward the bed, slides her hand under the mattress, and snatches the magazine from under it with two fingers.

I freeze in fright, jump to my feet, and try to get it from her, but she retreats, laughing, into her room.

"Maybe you want your mom to find this by accident?" she says, leafing through the magazine.

"Give it back," I sneer, but I'm in shock and I don't really know what to say.

"Must be quite exciting licking the paper . . ." she says, giggling.

She has everything, and I have nothing. She calls the shots.

"I'll keep this while you stand guard. If you spill the beans, I'll do the same," she says with cruel gentleness in her face, and closes the door.

Then they start to whisper and giggle on the other side of the door, and now and then they laugh out loud. They're leafing through the magazine and laughing because they know what I've been doing with it. My sins are public now, and I'll never be able to look anyone in the face again; I'm damned.

And the game starts behind the door.

"Ouch, Mike; stop, Mike; don't, Mike," she squeals, but she doesn't mean a word she says. The only thing that can be heard from him is snarling and growling.

Little by little, the sounds of her voice subside, the bed creaks like somebody is constantly sitting down and standing up, sitting down and standing up, and I can't pretend that this isn't interesting anymore. I go to the door, stand close, and listen. But I'm not going to stoop so low as to peek through the keyhole, just listen.

The human being is the only creature on the planet that is controlled by the hunger for sex alone. It's not like people are necessarily thinking about having babies—quite the contrary. The sexes use each other to fulfill their lust. The female puts on perfume and dresses so that most of her flesh is visible so the male gets water in his mouth and becomes mad with lust. The only thing humans have in common with other animals is the fact that it is the female who decides where and when this game takes place. And they never seem to get enough.

A long sigh comes through the door and is followed by some sort of neighing from Mike. Then I bend down to look through the keyhole. They are, however, still fully clothed, mostly anyway, but my cousin is lying under him and has her long legs hooked together behind his back.

"Do it," he hisses.

"No," she hisses back. "Not now. Not here."

Then I hear the rattle of keys by the front door. I bang the door vigorously.

"She's coming," I call, and keep looking through the keyhole.

Mike flies up from the bed, puts on his jacket and his shoes, opens the window, and carefully climbs out. I run to my window and see him jump from the drainpipe, sit on his bike, start it, and roar away.

Mom comes up the stairs and appears in the doorway, looking at me with astonishment.

"Are you awake?"

"I was just finishing doing math for school tomorrow," I say, and yawn. "But now I'm going to bed."

She says good night, turns off the light, and closes the door.

I sneak up to Gertrude's door and peek through the keyhole and watch her undress with a dreamy look on her face. She moves as if her head is shrouded in some strange fog. It takes her a long time to take off her leggings, stroking her hands down her legs, and finally she crawls under her comforter with a sigh of pleasure.

Chapter 25

The mind is a strange labyrinth, full of mysterious rooms with many pictures hanging on the walls, pictures of forests and castles, cities and mountains, oceans and dark, deep waters. And before you know it, you have disappeared into one of those pictures, into another world. And there is another time, different rules apply, and there are lots of people you've never seen, but still you know them well. And you talk to these people or walk silently by their side through green forest paths. And maybe there's a brook there and birds are singing in the trees. Before you know it, you have stepped out of the picture, back into the labyrinth, but then you're suddenly in another room with different kinds of pictures on the walls. And I'm not sure if all these rooms and these strange pictures are in my mind or if my life and my world are just another picture on a wall in somebody else's mind. Maybe there's a boy sitting somewhere, right at this moment, on a beach in Japan and another one high up in the mountains in India or in a forest in Italy. And I can meet them all in the rooms of my mind and sit by their side and talk to them and we understand each other because in the mind everybody speaks the same language. There, everybody is free.

I sit in my hollow for a long time, looking over the water, and time stands still. I'm waiting for my brother, the boy who used to be me, but he doesn't appear. Although I'm thinking about him, though I'm calling for him in my mind, I can't find him. I lack his courage. I still don't believe in miracles. And I still don't have enough faith in myself to walk on water.

I stand up and walk westward, jumping from rock to rock until I reach the sandy beach farther along the shore. The surf rolls up the sand, stretching its foaming fingers toward my feet. Above the beach is the road west, and I can hear the cars go by behind the bank. Once this beach was called the Money Beach, and Peter and I came here to find old coins that some bank had dumped on the beach, a long time ago, when the coins were out of use. We had to hack them free out of rusty clumps of iron that lay here and there on the sand. Some were made decades ago. Then we went to Peter's and sat there with some metal polish and cloths in our hands and rubbed them vigorously until they were as good as new. Those were the good days when life was simple.

That was the life that he led. The he who once was me.

And remembering this inspires me to look around for something exciting. There are lots of different shells glittering in the froth at my feet, shoes made of rubber with no soles underneath and boots buried halfway in the sand, floats from old nets, plastic cans, and shards of glass in all the colors of the rainbow, smooth and polished by the surf.

The foam from the wave weaves around my feet, and when it subsides, I see something glisten in the sand. I reach down and push the sand away as a large truck drives by on the road behind and honks its horn like a foghorn. It's a lock on a bag. It is the lock on my schoolbag. I dig my fingers in the sand, find the handle, and pull it out. The books are a chunk of wet mass, the ink has disappeared from the sheets of my notebooks, and the pages have turned to slime that drips from my fingers. I throw the books down in the hole that the bag has left, push the sand over, and pack it down with my foot. I thought that I had gained freedom by throwing my bag in the ocean and saying good-bye to everything. But I'm more a prisoner than anyone. I live in a lie, and I'm constantly on the run.

"To run away is not freedom. To fight, that's being free," says the voice in my head, and I know it's him. He led me here to the beach, exactly to the spot where my schoolbag had washed ashore.

"To fight," I say aloud, and sit in the sand with my schoolbag in my arms, looking at the surf tumbling onto the shore.

I take the back streets with the bag in my arms to avoid meeting anybody on their way home from school. Before I know it, I'm in Peter's neighborhood, behind the church. His dad's gray Chevrolet appears around the corner, and I'm forced to sneak into the yard and hide behind some bushes. Then I move slowly toward the dovecote and hide behind it, watching the car glide into the parking space.

Peter sits in the front seat, and when he steps out, it seems like he's looking toward the dovecote, like he knows I'm here. Did he see me run and hide? Jonathan strokes the paint on the hood of the car and says something to Peter that I don't quite hear.

But I hear Peter say, "No, it wasn't me."

"Well, somebody has been scratching the paint," Jonathan says angrily.

"It wasn't me," Peter says.

"Look at that," Jonathan says, and points at the hood.

Peter comes closer and looks at the hood and then at his father.

"Cleaning the car is your responsibility," Jonathan says forcefully, but Peter just looks down. "Are you telling me the girls did this?"

Peter doesn't answer.

"Right, that says everything, doesn't it? This is not like you, Peter. It costs money to fix these things. Well, it will be your job to polish this, young man," his father says, raising a finger. "I'll have to get the whole hood painted again now, and I don't have money for that. How long has it been like this? You better start at once before the rust sets in."

Jonathan goes into the house, cursing, and slams the door behind him. Peter fetches the car polish and some rags from the basement, and he's out again before I can sneak away. I watch him dip a rag into the polish and smear the thick substance onto the hood, but every once in a while, he looks in the direction of me and the dovecote. His father appears in the window, knocking on the glass, pointing, and Peter bends close over the hood, polishing as thoroughly as he can. When his father has disappeared from the window, Peter jolts and runs half-bent to the dovecote. I crouch down to the ground, making myself as small as possible, and stop breathing. I hear him come closer, panting and puffing.

"Are you there?" he whispers.

I'm silent as a mouse, determined not to be found out.

"Are you there, you fool?" Peter hisses on the other side of the dovecote. "You have to come out. Dad's home."

I'm trying to figure out why it should be of any concern to me that his dad is home; after all, it wasn't me who scratched the paint on the hood. But then I hear a hoarse voice drawling from within the dovecote.

"Leave me alone."

I realize Alice, Peter's older sister, is inside the cote.

"Are you drunk?" Peter whispers, obviously very upset.

"Oh, shut up," says the voice. "Let me sleep."

These words are followed by moaning and sighing like she's making herself more comfortable, rolling around in her den.

"Why did you have to scratch the car?" Peter whispers, reprimanding. "You know he loves that damn car. And now I have to polish it and probably pay for the damage as well."

"Can you please leave me alone?" the tired voice from inside the dovecote answers back.

"Hurry to the basement and take a shower there," he orders in a whisper. "Alice, please! Supper's in half an hour.

197

If you're not there, I'll—" But he is cut off by Jonathan's voice from the balcony.

"What are you doing there, Peter?"

"Nothing," Peter says innocently, and his voice suddenly becomes childish. "I thought I saw a loose board here," he says, and pretends he's fixing the cote.

"Have you finished polishing?"

"Nearly."

"Well, hurry up," Jonathan says, and disappears from the balcony into the house.

Peter kicks the dovecote and curses in a low voice, then runs to the car and starts to polish again as fast as he can, circle after circle on the hood, so that sweat pours from his brow.

A long, tired sigh comes from the dovecote. And after a little while, I hear low snoring.

Finally Peter finishes polishing the hood and runs into the basement, and I use the opportunity to back hurriedly out of the tangled bushes, crawl over a stone wall, and then run down the street.

When I open the door, it looks like nobody's home. Mom is not in the living room sewing or in the kitchen preparing supper. I open her bedroom door, and she is lying with a wet towel on her forehead. She looks away when the light falls into the dark room.

"Where were you?" she whispers to the wall.

"At Peter's," I say. "Are you sick?"

"I've got a terrible migraine. I'm afraid you'll have to help yourself to something to eat, bread or something."

"OK, don't worry," I say.

"Trudy isn't home yet," she says. "I don't know why she's so late."

When Mom has a migraine, I tiptoe around because her hearing becomes oversensitive and every sound pierces her head. I curse the sound of every car that drives down the street, making the glass tremble in the windowpane, because the smallest sound is like having a nail jammed into her head.

"Do you need anything?" I whisper.

"Maybe if you could chill the towel for me," she says.

I hold the towel under the ice-cold stream in the bathroom sink until my fingers are numb. Then I wring it out a little, tiptoe back into her room, and place it carefully on her forehead. She sighs with relief, and the light in the hallway falls gently across her face; her skin is smooth and pale, and her hands are white.

"Your dad called," she says, and closes her eyes as a single drop runs from the towel down her temple and disappears into her dark hair. "He wanted to talk to you. You can call him if you like."

I go into the hall and sit by the phone, looking at the number. I put my finger on the keypad and punch in the number without picking up the phone. Then I wait for a while, lift the handset, and put it back down.

"No answer," I whisper into her room, and she sighs and turns her head to the wall.

I sit at my desk and look at the falcon, then place both hands on the base and turn it slowly. The fanned wings touch my face lightly, and its open beak gapes at my forehead. I wish it was alive. Then I'd set it free. And it would fly all the way to the country, where the hills go on for so many miles that it takes days to walk across them, where the lake is so deep you could never reach the bottom. I wish.

What happened to Alice? Why did she lock herself in the dovecote? Was she playing truant like me, being a troubled child, a black sheep? What problems can there possibly be in her life, with her family? I can't imagine what they could be. Alice should know how I've been feeling. I didn't start smoking or drinking, even though I felt really bad. She's just a kid, a child. But maybe that's the problem.

To actually cease being a child, that's probably the greatest experience in life. But when do you become an adult, and when do you cease to be a child? Maybe life is not a journey along a straight road, from childhood to adulthood, like I thought, but a round trip from one cradle to the next one, until finally you are laid to rest in your grave, like a sleeping infant. Maybe you are not meant to cease being a child altogether, but rather to become a better child as you grow older. And maybe you can't truly be considered an adult until you have become a perfect child.

Chapter 26

"Wake up, Josh," somebody whispers into my ear, and at once I jerk up, staring into the pitch darkness. I can't see a thing and don't know where I am.

The shadowy figure of my cousin is moving by the bedside.

"Are you awake?" she whispers.

"What time is it?" I ask.

"I don't know. It's night," she says.

I reach for the bedside lamp and push the button. As soon as the light is on, she covers her face and turns away. There are red marks on her forearms, and her shirt is torn in two places; her hair is a mess. She smells of tobacco and alcohol.

She lowers her hands from her face, squinting at the lamp, eyes swollen from crying, mascara running down her cheeks. She's trembling.

"Can I talk to you a little?" she whispers. "I'm so cold."

She lies down on the bed beside me, hiding her face in my pillow.

"What happened?" I ask.

"Would you turn out the light?" she pleads into the pillow.

I reach over her and push the button, and she grabs my hand in the darkness and squeezes it tightly.

"Can I lie here for a while?" she says.

I move to the wall to make space, but she comes close to me, squeezing my hand. She sniffs vigorously, but then she lies silent for a long time, with the occasional sob and a sigh.

Little by little the events of the night gradually unfold, sometimes in a hoarse whisper, sometimes with long intervals between words. Then she utters a long sentence in a single flow, pushing it out as if she's retching.

She'd gone to a party with Mike, and the place was full of people, all older than her, and they were drinking and Mike wanted her to drink, but it was home brew and she didn't like it and didn't drink much at all. Then Mike wanted them to go into a room to fool around, and she didn't mind because she was bored anyway. But Mike locked the door and wanted her to undress. But she wouldn't, not in a strange house, in a strange bed. But he just got even more excited.

"He tore my skirt," she blurts out into the pillow, and her shoulders shudder. Then she says nothing for a long while. I can't say anything either. I touch her hair gently and pat her lightly and place my hand between her shoulder blades, feeling her heart beating hard into the palm of my hand.

"It hurt so much," she says, and squeezes my hand. "I've never done it before, and that's the honest truth, although you might not believe it. He was so worked up, he didn't listen to me at all—he wouldn't. What will I do if I'm pregnant?"

As soon as she has burst this last bit out, she starts to cry in earnest into the pillow, and I worry that she'll wake up Mom, who has a migraine and can hear everything. So I shush in a low voice, stroking her back, and pull the comforter over her. Then she moves closer to me and puts one arm around me, holding my hand tightly with her other hand and snuggling up to my chest.

"You're so kind to me," she says.

I can't say anything except, "There, there," like Mom did when I was little and she was comforting me. No, I have nothing to say. But my cousin has made me her confidant in the middle of the night, given me a portion of a terrible secret, and that's why I fill up with overwhelming affection. Suddenly she's just a little girl, a stupid kid who was lured into a trap. And I'm the only one she can trust in the darkness of the night. Poor Trudy. Just a little child, but inside a woman.

Chapter 27

The fire between the black rocks devours the pages one after the other, and the naked bodies writhe in the flames until they turn black and singed; the grimaces of lust change into astonished terror as the paper burns to ash that flies up from the rocks and out over the bay. Never again shall these demonic vampires keep me awake. I feel dirty and unclean having touched these pages. Is there any difference between my fantasies and what Mike did to Trudy? There's a thin line between thought and action. If I'd kept on how I was, I might well have turned into what Mike is, a sex-crazed barbarian and a soul murderer.

Now my cousin lies in bed with a cut lip and her soul in shreds. That's not love; that's for sure. What Mike did is something completely different and has nothing to do with love.

I sit in my hollow and watch the ashes blow over the rocks, up in the air, out onto the bay. If I hadn't played hooky from school I never would have found out that Trudy had a boyfriend. Then there never would have been a conspiracy between us, and maybe we would have continued being enemies. And if we'd been enemies, then she wouldn't have come to me in the night and trusted me with this terrible secret. Maybe she would have jumped into the harbor—who knows? Yes, maybe my existence on this planet has actually saved a life, because I played hooky. Then wasn't it a good thing that I did it?

I can almost hear my little brother's laughter echo off the rocks around me, and it feels as if he's looking at me with a teasing grin on his face.

"But why were you playing hooky?" it seems he's asking.

"Because I was scared," I say to the rocks.

"Of what?" asks the echo.

"Of myself, of everything. Afraid that I wasn't good enough, not fun enough, not handsome and terrific, not strong and wise. Then there was the pubic hair," I add.

"Of course that's the end of the world?" he says teasingly.

"It could well be, I'll tell you."

"But could it not be the beginning of a new world? A world where you don't have to be scared anymore, where it doesn't matter if you're handsome or terrific, where it's nobody's business if you are strong or wise, a world where the only thing that matters is for you to be as you are, not like anybody wants you to be."

"But who am I really?" I shout, and the question echoes over the bay.

For a long time, there is no reply except the sleepy lapping of the waves. The fire is almost out. But then the answer comes to me, not in words, because the voice is now silent, but it feels as if he's standing behind me, the he who used to be me and will always be there when I need him.

The answer trickles through my body like a warm stream, and I feel the fright subside and the anxiety melt away. I am unique, not like anybody else, perfect as I am. Whatever others say or think doesn't concern me anymore. It will be their words and their thoughts, not mine. To be free is not to run away. I'm going to fight for myself and stand by myself. I'm going to walk on water. Large warm drops of the first real spring rain hit the rocks all around me. At first like a light applause. I lean forward from under the rock and stand up straight, looking around me. I can feel his eyes upon me as the applause grows louder, and I know instantly that we'll never speak again, for now I'm ready to face the world on my own. Somewhere out there among the roaring noise of millions of heavy raindrops hitting both rock and sea, I just barely hear his faint whisper: "You'll be all right."

Chapter 28

A huge car is parked by the front door, so well polished that the rain runs off it immediately. I can even see my reflection in the dark-red paint. Mom is obviously home, because her coat is hanging by the door and her wet boots are on the doormat. I hadn't expected her to be home just yet, and I haven't quite prepared my speech, but that doesn't matter. I am as ready as I will ever be. Tonight I'm going to talk with Mom honestly. Tell her that I've been playing hooky, but now that's over and done with. I'm going to confess all my sins to her and ask her forgiveness, because the truth is the best you can do. But then I notice unfamiliar large black galoshes on the shoe rack.

"Josh? Is that you?" Mom calls from the living room.

"Yes," I answer, wiping my soaking-wet face, the water dripping off my drenched clothes all over the doormat. The days of lying and cheating are over. Today I'm baptized to the truth; I am the son of truth, its patron saint.

That's how I walk toward the living-room door: soaked to the bone but elevated in spirit.

I step over the threshold onto the gray carpet. I look toward Mom, sitting at the dining table, and I am nailed to the floor.

My mother is holding a typed letter in one hand, but with the other one she covers her mouth. Opposite her sits a bald man with horn-rimmed glasses, in a gray suit and white shirt with a red tie. He has placed his hat on the table beside the floral coffee cup from Mom's finest collection, which is never taken out of the cupboard except for the most honored guests.

"How do you do, Josh," he says in a mild voice. "We've been missing you at school."

As his voice hits my eardrums, I wonder if all strength will wither away from me. I wait for an excuse to roll out of my mouth, but my lying days are over. Mom looks at me with horror in her eyes like I'm not her son but some insect that's crawled out on the living-room floor and the only thing to do is to squash it into the carpet and vacuum the leftovers.

"How could you do this to me?" she whispers.

I've never heard this tone in her voice before, and it's like an ice-cold paw locks itself around my heart and squeezes it slowly apart.

"How dare you!" she screams out, and hits her flat hand on the table on top of the letter, so the fine china jumps on the flower-painted saucer. Pinko is startled and jumps in his seat.

"We shouldn't blame the boy too hastily," he says in a serious manner, pushing a finger lightly under the rim of his glasses; then he clasps his hands together and places them heavily on the table.

He's very calm where he sits opposite Mom, like our living room has become his office all of a sudden, and my mom and I just an inconvenient disturbance on a busy day.

"He's not the first kid to ever skip school," he adds, and pulls a chair from under the table.

"Come and sit here, Josh."

I sit down and take a deep breath.

"There are always some reasons for children to run way from school," says Pinko in an encouraging tone of voice to Mom. "And it is among my duties to find those reasons and eliminate them so everybody feels better. And of course we all want our Josh here to feel good about school, don't we?"

Mom doesn't reply, but I feel her eyes on me with the same look as before.

"Now, tell us what happened, Josh," Pinko says. "Was someone bullying you or teasing you? If someone has been bad to you, then you must tell me. We can't have anyone getting away with that kind of thing."

But these questions are not easily answered, for surely I was being bullied and teased, but it wasn't deliberately toward me, not in that sense. And even the things that had been done to me weren't that overwhelmingly terrifying that they justified running away from school. My thoughts go around and around at tremendous speed. One by one, they gradually fly into infinity, and there's nothing left in my mind except black empty space.

"You can trust that everything you say is strictly

confidential and won't go any further. It will only be between you and me," he says, and his voice echoes between the empty walls in my mind.

But then, a thin ray of light is thrown into the void and it falls on the slimy grim face of a bullfrog. At once I remember why I ran out of the shower room, promising myself never to go back to school. I know full well that it's not likely that Pinko will accept this as a fair reason, but it's the true reason.

"I am, I was, afraid of the shower warden."

"You mean Sandra?" he asks, surprised.

"I was afraid she was going to eat me."

For a second everything is still and nobody says a word. The headmaster's face doesn't move, except his chin drops a little and he blinks a couple of times, glancing sideways at Mom. She lowers her hands slowly into her lap, where they lie quite still, palms turned upward. She breathes out slowly as if she had been holding her breath. If she felt I was an insect before, I can't imagine what she thinks of me now.

"God help you, child," Mom mutters.

They straighten up in their seats, the chairs creak a little, and they glance at each other. I notice something boiling in Mom's throat, but Pinko just breathes out of his nose for a long time, resting his eyes on his clasped hands.

"A lie!" Mom screams in a clear voice. "You just tell stories! Tell lies! That's all you do. What am I supposed to do with you?" she shouts.

"Calm down, please be calm," Pinko says, taking control. "Hysteria doesn't help," he goes on. "Quite the opposite. Discipline. Josh is a creative boy and lets his imagination get the better of him. It's not at all uncommon. He just needs to learn to distinguish between illusion and reality."

Mom sniffs into her hand and struggles to hold back her tears. Pinko stands up, walks over to me, places a heavy hand on my shoulder, and bends down to me. There's a tone of disbelief in his voice regarding my statement, but still he is trying to figure out what really happened.

"What did she do?" he asks.

Conscious of my promise to the voice of truth, with the words already lined up on my tongue I start to speak. "Nothing," I say, looking straight at Mom. "I was just afraid."

Mom throws up her hands and laughs on the verge of tears, but Pinko straightens up slowly, takes his hand off my shoulder, and runs it over his bald head.

"Well," he finally says. "That's that."

He takes his hat off the table, and his fingers run over the brim of the hat for a while where he stands by the sewing machine.

"I want you to come back to school tomorrow," he says gently but firmly. "We won't let this interruption affect your studies. Easter is getting closer, and you'll have some extra work to do over the break. Then we'll see. Thank you for the coffee," he says, and is obviously relieved that this is over.

"And don't worry too much, Mrs. Stephenson," he adds. "Young boys need discipline, and it's the responsibility of the school to provide it."

Mom leads him to the door, and I hear them whisper for a while. Then she closes the front door, and I hear him walk down the path, hear him open the car door, slam the door, and start the engine. Its rumble drones in my ears until the car glides slowly down the street and the sound disappears.

I'm ready for Mom to come back into the living room hurling herself at me like a thunderstorm, but nothing like that happens. I hear her sit down in the kitchen, and after a little while I smell cigarette smoke. Mom never smokes on her own. I can't hear it, but I think she's crying. I haven't seen her cry since Dad left us. She probably cries silently so nobody knows of her sorrow.

That's how all the moms with sons like me must cry. Without a sound. Because a son will hurt his mother more than other men, without even realizing it, without meaning to. It's like we can't help it. And that's why all the mothers are sitting just like this, all over the world, each in her own corner. When the day's work is done, when others have fallen asleep and they've said good night to everybody, they sit down in their kitchens, maybe with a cup of coffee and a cigarette, and cry silently so nobody will guess their sorrow. And it doesn't matter how earnestly I ask her forgiveness in my mind, it's no use. I've broken her heart, and now I've got to mend it.

* * *

I'm almost asleep when Trudy tiptoes across the floor and sits on my bed.

"Can we chat a little?" she asks, and lies down, putting her head on the pillow.

Then she's silent for a while.

"Why did you do it?" she finally asks.

I don't know if it'll help explaining it to her, not sure if I know the answer anymore.

"You know," I say. "Just wanted peace. To be alone."

She turns over to me in the half-light, and her brown eyes gleam. Behind her, on the other side of the room, the curtains are half open and the glow from the lamppost seeps through the window. The light falls softly on her cheek, beside me on the pillow.

"You know very well the shower warden isn't a cannibal," she says. "You didn't really mean that, did you?"

"It wasn't just her. It was everybody. I just needed some time to think."

"You think too much," she says. "It's unhealthy to think as much as you do. Maybe you should write some poetry," she adds. "It gives your mind some rest. And your heart."

I smile in the twilight, but I don't answer.

"I love poetry," she whispers. "But there are so few boys who dare to be honest. Why are boys so strange?" she asks. "You think some guy is the man of your dreams and hope that he's kind too. But then he's just a brute. Why is everybody tying to be something they think other people admire? Why doesn't anybody want to be themselves?"

"I don't know," I say.

She's silent for a while, her thoughtful face lit up by the lamplight from outside.

"Maybe there is a good boy somewhere, just a normal boy, who would maybe have known how to love, who would have written poems for me. But I didn't see him because those boys always fall in the shadow of the others."

We lie side by side in silence for a long time, and I understand what she means.

"Do you think Dad was one of the others?" I ask.

"I don't know," she says. "I was so little when I saw him last, I wasn't thinking things like that then."

"Don't you find it strange," she says after a while, "that sometimes it's like you're alone in the world? You have parents and friends as well, good friends even, but still you're utterly alone."

I look at the soft pool of light that envelops Trudy and me, and wonder at how two souls can be so alike, when we're so different from each other in every other way. So this is how she thinks, just like me. And here I was, believing that nobody in the world had the same thoughts as me.

"Will you promise me one thing?" she asks.

"What's that?"

"Promise me that when you have a girlfriend, just be who you are and don't try to be anything else. Just so she knows that there's one good boy in this world."

Chapter 29

Mom walks me almost up to the school gates, just like on my first day, six years ago. Dad had just left, and she couldn't walk me all the way because of the prying eyes of the happy parents who would notice she had been crying. I'm carrying her old schoolbag because mine is ruined and she can't afford to buy me a new one after buying new books and notebooks. The shouting and the screaming from the school yard don't disturb me. I'm not afraid, but I'm not at ease, either.

Mom stops and looks at the school yard for a while. I stand by her side and wait. She hasn't told me off, not a word.

I wait for her to leave, and I wonder if I should say "Good-bye" or "I'm fine from here," but I don't want her to think that I feel like hurrying, like I'm ashamed of her or something.

"You have your lunch?" she asks.

"Yes," I reply, a little surprised because she put it in my bag.

"And your books?"

"Of course," I say, but still she stands there as if she wants to say something, tell me something.

"Well, I'll be home at the usual time, but there's food in the fridge."

Suddenly, the shrill school bell rings and I feel the anxiety knot tighten in my stomach.

"I have to go now, Mom."

"I talked to your father," Mom blurts out.

I look at her, astonished. Is she really going to tell me off right now? But then I notice she's not angry; her voice is not trembling. Her cheeks are blushing a little, and somehow her face looks younger.

"Did you tell him?" I ask.

"Of course I told him what's been going on. He is your father. Maybe he understands all this better than I do. What do I know about what thirteen-year-old boys are going through? He'll call you soon to have a chat," she says. "Go on, now, don't be late."

I run toward the school yard and then turn at the gates. Mom walks slowly down the street. Not in a straight line but carelessly wandering from side to side like she's not in a hurry, like she's enjoying herself, like a happy child playing in the twilight of the morning. She called him after six years of silence. And now she's free.

Pinko gives me a significant nod, then he leans against the corner of the teacher's desk and reads our names out loud. Peter isn't here; his seat is empty.

"Does anyone know about Peter?" Pinko asks, but nobody

knows anything. "Let's hope he hasn't been infected with the hooky disease," Pinko says, smirking. Half-muffled giggles are heard here and there around the classroom, and I feel my face turn red as blood. Then math begins, but fortunately Pinko leaves me alone and asks me nothing. My class is obviously way ahead of me, so there's no point calling me up to the blackboard. But then, Pinko does tend to call up those who aren't so good. Just so he can show us how wise he is, just to scare the stupid ones into working harder at their homework. I don't know why he does this. But I know this one thing: next time he calls me up to the blackboard, I'll have my revenge on him. I feel my anxiety subside, and suddenly I don't give a damn what anybody thinks about me. And I can't wait for Pinko to call me up. But it won't happen today.

In class with Miss Wilson, Tommy throws a couple of paper balls at my head out of habit. I peek over my shoulder and look at Clara, but then she looks up and our eyes meet for a split second. I look away instantly. She seems to have grown and matured since last I saw her; she's almost a woman, and more beautiful than ever. My face warms up and the sweat starts to run, gluing the shirt to my back.

It's not until lunchtime, while everybody is outside and I'm certain that nobody is in the hallway and I'm alone in the classroom, that I take a bundle wrapped in brown paper out of my schoolbag. It's tied with a thick string and for safety I've also wrapped it in Scotch tape. I move slowly around the classroom toward her desk, not taking my eyes off the door. If someone sees me, I'm lost forever. Finally I stand by her desk and lightly brush my fingertips over the writing on the page of her notebook, her pen, her pencil case. Her schoolbag sits beside the desk. I press the lock, and it opens with a gentle click. My heart is beating fast. The scent of her pours out of the bag, and in between textbooks and notebooks is her colorful silk scarf that she had around her neck this morning. I take it out and press it to my face, breathing in her scent, which I haven't smelled since I made her fall over in the playground chasing her. I want to kneel here on the floor and keep on breathing in until there's no scent left in the scarf. But when I hear running footsteps outside, I wrap the scarf around the bundle, thrust it into her schoolbag, and run for my seat. On the other side of the door, I hear the girls chatting and laughing while they take off their coats. When they enter, I pretend to be reading with my face down in a book. Now my heart is wrapped in brown paper inside her schoolbag. Before the day is over, it will be completely at her mercy.

The bell rings for the last time; the drumbeat of running feet on the stairs fills my ears as I run along with the others into the fresh afternoon. The boys suddenly surround me, and, as usual, Tommy is the leader.

"Were you playing hooky?" he asks, and the boys giggle behind him.

"Why do you say that?" I ask.

"Nobody has fever for such a long time," Tommy says. "And then you started to cry in front of Sandra the shower warden." The boys laugh. "We all heard you. Then you just ran out, still in your gym shorts," he says, and the boys are all eyes and ears, waiting for some pathetic excuse that they can ridicule.

"You know meningitis?" I say in a serious voice. "You can die from it." I look them all in the eye with a grave face.

They calm down a little, and Tommy gives me a nod of respect, like I just scored a beautiful goal.

"That's horrific, man," he says, and punches me lightly on the shoulder. "Cool," he adds.

The bells are ringing in the church tower. The clear sound travels over the neighborhood and vibrates in the air. Two ravens are circling the tower; they sit on the roof, fly up again, and finally rest on a column at the top of the tower. Their crowing, hollow and chilling, echoes in the walls of the houses that surround the church hill.

I cut down the alleyway, and as I get closer to Peter's house, I see there's a light on in almost every room, which is unusual because his father is really strict on saving energy.

I walk into the yard, and there's Peter, standing with a huge sledgehammer raised up high in the air. He's completely out of control. He is slamming it furiously at the roof of the dovecote. The wood creaks under the heavy blows. He's wearing just his pajama pants, barefoot, hacking away like mad. He doesn't hear me when I call his name but goes on hitting the dovecote. There's an uncanny violence in his auburn hair and his back and in the way he moves. I've never seen him like this before. The ridge of the cote starts to give way, lower and lower until the roof collapses with a loud crash. Peter hits the walls with the sledgehammer without hesitating or slowing down, like a machine, like it's a matter of life and death, that the cote be smashed to pieces, leveled to the ground this minute, so nobody will know it ever stood there. The wooden handle slides in his palms; he raises it up high and grunts angrily with every blow. The walls begin to cave in, and the thin wire net rips apart. Boards break in two, and there's a loud crack.

"Peter!" I shout, and walk into the yard.

He turns quickly with the sledgehammer held high as if he's ready to knock out anyone who tries to stop him. This is not the Peter I know. His face is boiling, his eyes shooting fiery sparks from under the darkness of his brows.

"What?" he cries, and I'm not sure if he even recognizes me. His lips are a straight line and he's blue in the face.

"What's wrong?" I ask, not daring to move closer.

"What do you want?" he screams, and raises the sledgehammer threateningly.

"Peter, what happened?" I scream back, and feel his madness affecting me.

But then he finds his bearings and lowers the sledgehammer a bit. His face goes slack, his bare chest heaves, and his lips are trembling.

"She's in the hospital," he cries out.

"Who?" I demand.

"Alice," he shoots back.

Then he lets go of the sledgehammer, its heavy head sinking into the wet grass, and grabs a fistful of his auburn hair, pulling it from his scalp.

"They didn't know a thing; they didn't want to. I found her downtown, behind a trash can. She was almost frozen through," he says, and his voice breaks, and he dries his nose with a swift movement, then he goes on pulling at his hair.

"I barely managed to get her home," he says. "And I put her in the shower in the basement and turned on the hot water, but she didn't wake up."

He's silent for a while and stares at the ground.

"Then I went and woke them," he says. "It couldn't go on any longer; I had to let them know. I thought she was dead. She just lay in the shower completely limp and didn't move. And Dad!" he says, and spits. "He just started to yell at her when she was maybe even dead! And it was me," he screams with tears running down his face, hitting his clenched fist on his chest, "it was me who had to call the ambulance. Me!"

As soon as he has said the word *ambulance,* he covers his face with both hands, like a little boy pretending to hide. His whole body trembles.

"Why is he always like that to her?" he asks into the palms of his hands. "She hasn't done anything to him. Why is he such a prick?"

I stretch to touch him, but when I place my hand on

his shoulder, he jolts and rips the sledgehammer from the ground, turns around, and pounds away on the heap of wood.

"*Stop it, Peter!*" I shout.

"*I can't,*" he screams back. "*I'm so angry, angry, angry!*"

The sledgehammer smashes the wood, the splinters flying all around him. Finally he stops and stands there, almost out of breath, panting, looking at the ruins of the dovecote. Then he sniffs vigorously.

"I'm cold," he says. "I'm going in now."

"Is someone at home?" I ask.

"I'm babysitting the little one," he says. "Mom and the others are at the hospital."

We stand side by side, looking at the ruins at our feet, and his breath slows down and the stillness in the garden is thick, enveloping, gentle. He lets go of the handle of the sledgehammer, and it falls into the shimmering wet grass with a low thud.

He turns away without looking at me, padding barefoot and exhausted across the wet lawn, stumbling down the steps to the basement, and disappears into the house.

The church bell rings out a bright note, and the ravens fly silently into the sky.

Chapter 30

There's a large photograph on the front page of the morning paper. It shows a tiny black child in the arms of a fat white nurse. Beside the nurse is the child's skeleton of a mother. She is kneeling in the yellow sand beside the nurse, holding the child's limp fingers. The white nurse is embracing the child, holding him tight to her large breast. The nurse is looking very sad because the child is dying while the photographer is taking the picture. Although dying from hunger is a horrible way to die, still this child dies in a beautiful way, because it dies in somebody's arms. There are children in this country who starve as well, maybe not from hunger, not because the harvest was ruined or because of drought or floods or wars. Here children die without anyone noticing it. They die silently on the inside, but the body is condemned to go on living, forced to pretend that everything is fine, while the dusty corpse of the soul dries up. Everybody pretends that nothing is wrong, just like Peter's parents did while Alice was crumbling in their midst, like a flower without water. I wish the parents of this world had the courage to embrace their children and tell them, "I'm here for you because you're my child. And when I'm not with you any longer, you will know that I have loved you."

I'm a little bit anxious about Dad calling tonight. Maybe he won't call until tomorrow. I hope he'll just forget as usual. Mom said I could take the phone into my room if I wanted to. The cord isn't long enough to reach the desk—it only reaches the bed—so I put the phone on the bed and close the door. Then I sit at my desk and struggle on with my homework. I want to call Peter to ask if everything is all right, but I don't. There's nothing I can say that would matter, anyway.

I wrestle with my math exercises under the watchful eye of Christian the Ninth. Trudy has gone to bed. She's going to school tomorrow. Mike has called twice, but she hung up on him. Mom doesn't know anything about what happened, and I don't think Trudy will ever tell her. She seems to be over it; at least she no longer wakes up in the middle of the night to come over to my bed for a chat. I kind of miss that, though. Everything changed when she was sure that she wasn't pregnant. That night she slept like a log. I'm fairly sure that it's going to be a long time before she gets another boyfriend. That much is obvious.

Algebra is the most incomprehensible thing in the world. Why can't you do math with words instead?

$$(boy + girl) \times love = disappointment$$

$$(heart + heart) + love \div teenager = disappointment$$

It makes no difference how I arrange this problem; the result is always disappointment. But maybe I'm not putting this together right; maybe what's wrong is the word *love*, because without love there wouldn't be disappointment.

I'm absorbed by this new mathematical theory of mine and have long forgotten my unsolved algebra problems that Pinko gave me this morning, when suddenly the phone rings behind me. I jump to my feet and knock my notebook off the desk to the floor. The black telephone lies heavily on the soft comforter. Before it rings again, I've sat on the bed, raised the earpiece, and placed it by my ear.

"Hello, Josh," my dad says.

"Hello," I say.

"What are you doing?" he asks.

"Math," I reply.

"I see. That's good."

"Yes," I say.

"So, son," he says. "So that's what you're doing."

"Yes," I say.

He clears his throat, and then he's silent for a while. There's some strange eagerness in his voice when he starts to talk again, not anger or anything like that, but like he honestly wants me to know that he understands completely.

He says that Mom told him what happened. He says it was a real surprise because he thought I was happy at school and with Mom; he hadn't imagined anything else. But then he says he started to remember how difficult and unfair life could seem when he was my age. How passing remarks could hurt and small problems seemed insurmountable. He says that he started to remember things that he thought he had forgotten long ago.

He goes on talking as if he is not in a hurry at all. His voice is easy and warm, and I hold the earpiece close to my ear and listen to every word. He starts to tell me about when he was my age and played hooky himself. He took Granddad's little boat and rowed out, because he wanted to be a sailor like Granddad. He saw no use in hanging around in a classroom when the sun was shining over the blue water of the big lake. When Granddad heard about it, he didn't say anything.

"But the next morning, he woke me up at four o'clock, ordered me to get going, and all that day we were hauling the nets on his motorboat. When we came ashore, he ordered me to fillet the catch, and when that was over, he sent me to the fishing sheds and told me to stay there until he came to fetch me. And there I stood, long into the evening, threading the bait on the hooks on the line until I could no longer feel my fingers and was dreaming about going back to school. He did exactly the same thing the next day and the day after until I gave in and pleaded with him to let me go back to school."

"Was Granddad always so mean?" I ask.

"He knew it wouldn't work to tell me anything. I had to figure it out for myself. And I certainly did after those three days."

Then he's silent, and for a while, I hear only the low buzz on the line and look at Christian the Ninth on my desk, illuminated by the light from the lamppost outside.

"How was the checkup, by the way?" I ask, hoping to keep this conversation going for as long as I can.

He replies that he is fine now, and that he has resigned from the *Orca*.

"You know Suzy is expecting?" he says.

"Yes, I know," I say.

He says he owns a small motorboat and is going to do some fishing in the spring, because nothing is like being out on the boat on a fine bright morning. Then he's also been laying nets with another guy, and that's good money. And he's been fixing motors for some people and is thinking about starting up a small repair shop in the spring. Then he's silent for a while and clears his throat.

"It would be nice to have a helping hand around here with this and that," he says. "I'll need to paint the boat soon. Then there's a lot to do when a child comes into the world."

"Yes," I say. "I guess so."

"Would you maybe like to try and spend some time with me?" he asks.

"Me?"

"You haven't been here since you were a little boy, when your mother and I went to your granddad's funeral. Lots of people here are asking after you."

"About me?"

"Your cousins and aunties," he says.

"Really?"

"I'm sure you would love it on the boat with me. You don't get seasick, do you?"

"I don't know."

"You should have enough sailor's blood."

"I guess," I say.

We're silent for a while, and I hear down the phone that he lights his pipe. I can almost smell the scent of his tobacco. I close my eyes and imagine that we're sitting side by side in his house in the country, where the summer is so warm that you can run in your shorts all day long.

"When can I come?" I ask.

He hesitates for a second, and I hear him blow the smoke out slowly.

"Whenever you want, Josh. Whenever you want."

"When are you going to paint the boat?" I ask.

"Oh, I don't know. After Easter, I guess," he says.

"So soon?"

"As a matter of fact, I have to come to the city, right after Easter," he says. "There are things I need for the motor. Then I'm going back the next day."

"I see."

"If you want to come with me then," he says thoughtfully and hesitates, "well, then I guess I have to speak to your mom soon."

"Yes," I say. "I guess that's best."

"Well, son," he says. "It's settled then."

"Yes," I say.

We say good-bye and he hangs up, but I hold the phone in my hand for a long time, listening to the dial tone.

Chapter 31

Mom bids me good morning with a smile and strokes my hair like she used to before. This is the first time she's done this since Pinko visited. And like she used to, she hums along to the radio as she butters my sandwich while Trudy and I crunch our cornflakes. Then she puts on her coat and her hat, and then Trudy stands up. I can hear their footsteps on the path through the open kitchen window, and their voices grow fainter.

Peter's seat at school is still empty, and it worries me. I start to think what he must have imagined when my seat was empty day after day. I'm sort of considering running to his house at lunch, but then I notice all the girls have gathered around Clara's desk, whispering and shooting suspicious glances all over the classroom. Her girlfriends stand around, stretching the chewing gum out of their mouths, swinging it around their fingers, and putting it back into their mouths; then they make a series of cracking sounds, drag it out of the corners of their mouths again, then back in their mouths again, and then they chew with great speed. And now everything is said in secret whispers, and they glance with their suspicious eyes down the row of desks, scrutinizing each boy with their eyes and whispering in one another's ears. And then there's the occasional giggle. I'm on tenterhooks because I think I know what they're talking about. That's why I don't dare to move, because it could make me look suspicious. So I sit quiet as a mouse and eat my sandwich.

After school, I take the shortcut down the alleyway and go to Peter's. I ring the doorbell. His mom comes to the door, holding the little one in her arms, and from inside the house, I can hear Peter's younger sisters arguing. She looks tired but smiles and talks in a happy tone of voice like nothing at all has happened.

"Hello, Josh, dear. Such a long time since I've seen you. Are you better now?" she asks, and strokes my cheek briefly.

"Yes," I answer, but when she asks what was wrong with me, I have some difficulty answering, because somehow I can't lie to Peter's mom.

"It was just some kind of flu," I force myself finally to say.

"Well," she says, and gives me a warm smile, "it's good that's over then."

"Is Peter in?" I ask.

"No, he's not," she says, and her smile becomes somehow stiffer and her eyes a bit colder, like I insulted her in some way by asking.

"He went to visit our Alice at the hospital," she says. And suddenly I get the feeling that she's not at all comfortable answering me.

"She's a little sick," she explains so I won't go thinking that this is anything serious.

The little one starts to cry in her arms, and she shushes her gently and looks at me and puts her hand on the doorknob.

"I'll tell him you came by," she says, and closes the door.

I don't go home right away but take a long detour into the neighborhood where Clara lives. I stand on a corner and peek my head around the building. From here I can see her house, a large white-stone house with two floors and a flight of steps up to the front door. On the gable at the end facing me is a small balcony on the second floor. A woman pushes a stroller past me, and an old man in a black coat and a gray hat walks carefully on the sidewalk, slow and out of breath.

Finally I see her coming up the street along with her girlfriends. They're chatting and laughing and stand for a while outside her house. She's holding her bag in front of her with both hands, kicking it lightly with her kneecaps every now and then. I purse my lips and clench my fists in my pockets, peeking around the corner with one eye. Eventually they say good-bye, and she runs up the stairs and disappears into the house.

Her room must be the one with the balcony. In a castle like this, the princess surely has a room with a balcony so she can look over her realm and dream of the prince that will get it all, one fine day, along with her.

* * *

Peter stands on the doorstep when I open the door. He is almost the same as before, but there's something different about him. He salutes by raising his hand carelessly to his eyebrow, and instead of putting on the hard soldier face like usual, he just smirks and mumbles, "Reporting for duty, sir."

I smirk as well but don't salute. It's like we've both agreed to stop this childish nonsense.

He sits at my desk as usual and I on my bed.

"Mom said you came by," he says.

"Yeah, I came by," I say.

He becomes a little awkward, staring for a while at his hands, sighing and smirking.

"I was really mad the other day," he says without looking up.

"Yes," I say.

He looks over the desk as if to find something to fiddle with or to examine because he's not comfortable being the center of attention.

"How is Alice?" I ask.

"She's going to be fine," he says, and hesitates for a moment and takes a deep breath before all of a sudden blurting it all out.

"She fell in with a bad crowd. She was killing herself. I didn't know what to do and no one else knew and then this happened, but now she's going to be fine. They're all talking again, Dad and Alice and everyone, you know. And now everything is going to better, much better, you know, for all of us."

"Well, that's good, then," I say.

"Yes," he says. "It's very good."

Then he grabs a copy of *Tintin* and leafs through it, and I stand up to feed the fish.

"Hey, are you coming to the costume ball?" he says finally.

"Maybe," I say.

"Should I go as a gorilla?" he asks. "What are you going to go as?"

"I don't know," I say. "Haven't thought about it."

"Maybe I'll be too hot being a gorilla. You know, it's a bodysuit."

"Yes, maybe," I say.

"When do you think you'll decide?"

"You mean the costume?"

"Whether you're coming."

I can tell that he really doesn't want to go unless I go with him. So I decide to go.

"I guess I'll go."

"Great!" he says, obviously relieved. "Then we'll go together."

"That's fine," I say.

He laughs about something he sees in *Tintin*.

"We could be the Thomsons," he says, pointing at a frame in the book showing the hilarious detectives wearing some bizarre national costume.

We discuss it for a while, but finally Peter decides on the gorilla. And while we're sitting like this, talking, I can feel what has changed. He no longer knows best about everything. Whatever the reason, he is insecure and seems to find some support in me, like I used to in him.

The way things were before, that was another life, another existence. Peter puts down *Tintin* and gently strokes the wings of my falcon with his fingertips, the wings that once soared the skies, high above the earth. Now the falcon stands still on my desk. Somewhere out there at this moment, another falcon is stretching its wings, finding its freedom, just like I am, just like Peter will someday soon, I hope.

Chapter 32

The wooden floor creaks and cracks under our feet as we run around and around the old gym. Then the whistle blows, and we stop and form a line by the bars on the wall.

A short sharp whistle: hang on bar and raise legs.

We hang on the bars and raise our legs. Raxel inspects the line with his cane, poking the feet of those who have to raise them higher. We hang like this for a long time, our legs horizontal in the air, completely exhausted, until he blows the whistle again and we lower our legs. A couple more times, then we have a breather.

A whistle, and we jump over the pommel horse, again and again, run back around and get in line, jump again, over and over, running, jumping, running, jumping.

"Move it, move it," Raxel growls, and we move it. Out of breath and sweating, blue in the face.

Whistle: everybody sit down, and we sit.

Raxel draws out the ropes that hang from a sliding bar on the ceiling, and ten ropes dangle in front of us like cobras. There are two teams. We have to race against the other, up the ropes, hit the ceiling with our hands, back down, next. The teams line up, and the first two boys run for the ropes, jump at them, and start wriggling their way upward to the shouting and the screaming of the others.

I shout as well. This is exciting. It's also the last challenge of the class, and this is the last PE class before Easter.

The boys dangle on the ropes, heaving themselves upward, grip by grip, squeezing the rope with their bare feet. One of them lets out a loud cry as he slams the palm of his hand on the ceiling and then hurls down the rope as fast as he can, jumps on the floor, and runs to the line, where he hits the palm of the next one, who runs for the rope. We're clapping and stomping our feet in rhythm so the floor booms. I'm the last one in my team, holding my hand out, ready, set, go!

The floor creaks and groans under my pounding step as I run for the rope, then I jump on it, lock my fingers around it, fold my legs around it, and squeeze. The rope is swinging, soaking with sweat. I can't hear the shouting anymore, just my own heartbeat in rhythm with my hissing breath, thundering in my ears. I grab the rope tightly above my head and pull myself up, pushing with my feet. The rope burns the skin on my feet as I push faster, trying not to lose my grip on the rope. Grab, pull, push. Grab, pull, push. The ceiling gets closer and closer, and I squeeze the rope between my thighs and wrap it around my ankle as I stretch out my hand, screaming loud, hitting the ceiling of the old gym with the palm of my hand. At once I hear the stomping and the clapping and the shouting and finally, finally the triumphant scream from the damn whistle.

My heartbeat is still pounding in my ears when I sit on the bench in the locker room out of breath. Tommy is boasting about his achievements, claiming that he was the quickest one to climb the rope, and he could prove it if Raxel had used the stopwatch. Then he starts to run around naked as usual, trying to grab people's underwear to throw into the showers. Sweat is running all over me, and the only thing I can think about right now is standing for a long time under a hot shower, letting the stream cleanse me completely. I stand up and take off my pants and my shirt.

"What the hell?" Tommy shouts. "Would you look at this!"

I still have the shirt over my head, so I don't know what Tommy is referring to. When I've undressed, I see that Tommy is pointing at me and the boys are staring.

"What?" I ask.

"You're getting pubes, man!" Tommy yells, laughing, looking around like the leader of the crowd.

Some laugh with him, but the others sit awkwardly on the bench, blushing and groping for something in their sports bags.

"So?" I say.

"It's just so funny." He giggles, but the others are silent.

"It'll be awfully funny as well," I say as I walk to the showers, "when all of us are hairy as mammoths and you're still bald as a baby."

And with these words, I walk past dumbstruck Tommy and disappear into the showers to the explosive laughter of the other boys.

* * *

Carol, my fire-breathing auntie, sits in the kitchen with a cup of coffee, talking to Mom. I hear the conversation revolve around the dress that Mom is making her for the annual dinner dance. Carol is asking Mom to join her at the dance.

"Here he comes, the villain," Carol calls out when she sees me in the hall.

"Nice news I hear about you," she says when I enter the kitchen. Clouds of smoke twirl around her head.

I fetch the chocolate from the cupboard, put a few spoonfuls in a glass, and add cold milk. I don't know if she's waiting for an answer from me or not, and Mom says nothing as usual when Carol is here.

"Do you really have to smoke that much?" I say, and open the kitchen window.

"So! We're a moral preacher now, are we?" Carol chuckles. "You'd be hearing a word or two if you were my child," she adds.

I walk past them and stop at the threshold, stirring the cocoa in the glass.

"Yes, you would certainly know the meaning of discipline if you were mine," Carol says, and puts out her cigarette.

When I'm in the hall, I stop by the mirror and decide to say something that she cannot help but hear.

"I'd be smoking like a chimney too, if I were yours."

239

I hear Mom react and a sudden gasp from Carol, but I hurry up the stairs to my room, sit by my desk, and sip the chocolate milk.

After a while, I hear her say good-bye and leave. And then the sewing machine starts to buzz in the living room.

The winter after Dad left, Mom and I moved into a small apartment and slept in the same room. Sometimes I woke up beside her as she moaned and sighed from bad dreams, her hands working in the half-light, moving in thin air over the comforter. The hands of a working woman, hands of a mother. But she was the one who sat by my bed and fed me mashed bananas when I had the flu. She was the one who sat by my side after she picked me up from the playground, watched me draw, and listened to everything I had to talk about that was interesting to *me*. Surely she must have had more than enough on her mind. But still she sat by my side and listened. And she tickled me in her big bed until I was in fits of laughter and cuddled me and called me her little prankster. And she taught me beautiful prayers about Jesus and the angels and sang me songs and read me stories until I fell asleep from her soothing voice. She was like that.

Sometimes she was annoyed and tired. Sometimes she was angry and scolded me, usually not without good reason. And she believed blindly in Jesus and God's will to rule her life like a dictator. She sings far too loudly in church and lets Auntie Carol boss her around far too much. But that's how she is.

It was also she who called up my dad instead of punishing

me and told him that he had a son. That was her. And I know how hard it was for her to talk to him properly for the first time in six years, but she did it for me, since how else could my father have known how I was feeling?

The light from the little bulb on the sewing machine is the only light on her face where she sits running the material under the needle that ticks away.

I'm sitting in the old chair, watching her, ready to try the thing on when she tells me to. Just over thirteen years after the day of the great blizzard in the month of February, when the radio played "Love Me Do" and the midwife shouted, "You're not seriously thinking of giving birth in this weather, are you?" she is sewing a costume for the boy that God lent her, the boy who lied to her and cheated her. Once upon a time, she was young and free and had her dreams. Her heart full of hopes. And there were probably many who wanted to dance with her. But then Dad appeared, and there was no one else. Then I arrived. Then it was just me.

"Come here," she says softly, and I stand up straight. She helps me put on the jacket with a hump on its back.

"Why do you want to be a hunchback?" she asks absently, with pins in the corner of her mouth, fastening up the hem and folding up the sleeves to figure out the correct length.

"Like in the movie," I say. "Don't you remember?"

"Quasimodo?" she asks.

"Yes, Quasimodo."

"Well, dear," she says, and I notice she's hiding a smile. "Then you'll have to ask your cousin to paint your face or something, because you're not that ugly."

I nod, but I don't answer. I have some difficulty talking right now. I can only swallow a couple of times and purse my lips and stand here like a mannequin until she has marked all she needs to mark and takes the jacket off.

"There," she says with a gentle sigh, and sits down at her sewing machine, putting on her glasses. "Now you can go to your room. I'll manage from here."

Even though I really just want to sit here in the twilight and listen to the needle tick away, watch her face in the small light, listen to her movements, the rustle of the fabric and the wailing of the wind outside, I go to my room because she asks me to. Because from now on, I'm going to be a good boy.

Chapter 33

A couple of vampires with black top hats are striding across the street in the moonlight, accompanied by a tall mushroom. And from out of cars, elves and trolls appear, along with pirates and soldiers with machine guns, huge honeybees, cowboys, aliens, and knights.

Peter marches along beside me in a chicken costume. It turned out that the gorilla costume was too big for him. The top half of his beak points out from his forehead and the lower half from under his chin. He is wearing huge chicken feet and laughs hysterically every time he takes a step. He's completely immersed in character and adds a cluck both before and after everything he says.

Up on the ceiling, a disco ball is hanging, turning around, throwing white, blue, red, yellow, and green flashes from the stage lights through the darkened school hall, hitting painted faces and masks. The floor trembles along to the heavy bass from the speakers. Everybody here is something that they're really not, except for the teachers holding their hands over their ears with a smile, while monsters, animals, and famous people from history jump in the sweaty crowd, dancing like mad.

Up on the stage, two DJs are standing with their boxes full of CDs. They are gradually building up the tension with nonchalant looks on their faces. They're obviously the center of attention because they are fifteen or sixteen, with a cool air of indifference about them.

Tommy is determined to get all the attention as usual. He is wearing leopard-print swimming trunks and nothing else, playing King of the Jungle. He shows off his muscles on the dance floor, hits his chest, and yodels like Tarzan himself.

"I should have worn the pirate costume," Peter cackles by my side. "Being a chicken isn't that cool."

"But there are four pirates," I say. "At least you're the only chicken."

I can't sit straight because my hump juts out like a pyramid between my shoulder blades. Trudy used tons of her makeup to paint my face. My hair is sprayed stiff on end, and my eyebrows are pitch-black, one painted up on my forehead, the other a bit lower so my eyes look crooked on my face. Trudy dampened balls of cotton in makeup, sprayed them stiff, and stuck them to my face, to look like warts. I've got a small rubber ball up my left nostril, so my nose is crooked as well.

"You look terrible," Peter said when I came to his house. His parents and sisters laughed at us, even Alice. The house seemed still full of noisy children, a happy family again. But when Jonathan called after us, asking if he should pick us up after the dance, Peter called back, "No. We'll walk."

It was the only time tonight he didn't cluck either before or after the sentence.

Clara sings loudly with her girlfriends, and they turn and twirl so their gowns and silk scarves fly around them. She has glitter in her black hair, with red lips and painted eyes. Tommy is jumping around her like a monkey, and she flashes him a smile.

Yes. She's smiling at him.

Then the song is over, and she rushes through the crowd with her friends toward Peter and me. They're sweating and out of breath, and one of them asks if the chairs by us are free.

"Yes," Peter says, and clucks, and they laugh at him and sit down, but I look away, determined to make it look like I haven't noticed them.

"Who are you?" Clara suddenly asks, and turns to me.

But before I can answer, she's figured it out.

"My God! You're the cripple. Did you all see the movie? It was so sad. Cool costume. Who made it?"

"Mom," I say, and am about to add that it was actually my cousin who painted my face, but she's not listening.

"Look at Tommy! Is he for real?"

And she laughs at Tommy's foolish behavior on the dance floor.

"What's with you two?" she asks. "Why aren't you dancing?"

Then Peter starts to flap his wings and raise his feet high up and cluck, and the girls laugh. But Clara stands up and walks to me.

"Dance with me."

"Me? N-N-ow?" I stutter, and my face is boiling.

"C'mon," she says, and grabs my hand, and before I know it, I'm out on the dance floor for the first time in my life. The one I love is standing before me, and noise is pouring from the speakers and the floor is vibrating, but I'm frozen and can't move.

Everybody around me is moving. A jumping horde of fun, but I'm completely paralyzed and just want to run away.

"Why don't you dance?" she shouts.

"I can't. I don't know how."

"There's nothing to it!" she calls back reassuringly. "Just do like this!"

Then she swings lightly, and her movements are soft and self-confident. And I start to stomp my feet and feel like a rhinoceros stuck in the mud. Tommy is on the other side of the room, and I'm hoping he'll leave us alone. I'm sweating terribly, and the paint is starting to run down my face; one of my warts comes loose and dangles off my cheek. I'm soaking wet, and I don't look up, afraid that our eyes will meet. I shake and stomp and trample around, trying to move like everybody else. Suddenly she grabs my hand with her right hand but puts her left hand on my shoulder.

"There," she says. "Hold me."

And I do as she says and let her take control until I finally find the rhythm. Our fingers melt together, and the palm of my hand is resting on her back and our faces are so close that I can feel the heat from her. Her hair swings in front of me, filling my unblocked nostril with the most wonderful scent.

Then the song is over and I don't know what to do, so I stand still, holding her.

"You're sweating," she says.

"I know," I say.

"One of your warts is falling off," she says.

"I know," I say.

"Should I take it off?" she asks.

"Sure," I say, and she raises her hand from my shoulder, touches my cheek with her fingertips, takes the wart between them, and pulls it off.

"Did it hurt?"

"Oh, no."

"Should we dance some more?"

"Sure," I say, waiting, prepared for the noise to pour out again, determined to show her that I've figured out how to do this. But then the hall fills up with fragile guitar plucking and the low humming of a lazy brass band.

She embraces me, wraps her arms around me, and we're almost not moving at all.

The sweat glues our cheeks together, and her hair is in my face. I can feel her jaw move by my cheek as she sings softly with the music, whispering in my ear, and I close my eyes.

My lips are right by her ear, and I could so easily whisper something to her, anything, everything that I want and yearn to tell her right now. But I don't. I just melt, dissolve in this lovely embrace, and we're almost not moving at all.

Then the song fades out, she loosens her arms, throws her hair to the side, and gives me a smile, and her eyes twinkle like two wishing stones in a clear stream. I feel like I've fallen asleep. There's a white mark on her cheek from my cousin's makeup, and I'm about to stretch my hand out to wipe it off, an excuse for a touch, but at the same instant, she grabs my shoulders, moves quickly close to me, and kisses me with her open mouth.

The lights are lit in the hall, the DJs put a silly children's song on and think they're very funny, and by the time I've gathered my senses, she's gone, and I'm surrounded by cowboys, clowns, and vampires. Tommy is in the middle of the throng, looking in all directions, calling her name. The name of the girl who just kissed me.

Peter waddles through the crowd and takes a few giant chicken steps toward me.

"Are you coming?" he asks.

Trudy is on the phone when I come in. She's red in the face and hurries to finish the conversation when I close the front door. She tells me that Mom went to the dance with Carol, then she goes into her room. After a while, I hear music from her stereo. There's obviously a new boyfriend on the horizon. And for some reason, she's reluctant to tell me anything about it. But it doesn't matter because I know how she feels. Because I'm also busy trying not to explode into a thousand pieces or dissolve into thin air or melt down through the floor or something. I know she'll confide in me sooner or later, when she's ready. I look in the bathroom mirror at this beaming Quasimodo, the hunchback that has just been kissed by his Esmeralda. I feel like if I wash my face, the dream will go away, so I keep on staring in the mirror, at my lips that she kissed just moments ago. When the sweat has solidified on my body and the makeup is crumbling off my face, I turn on the shower, undress, and stand quite still under the hot stream for a long time.

I find it almost impossible to fall asleep. My body is filled up with a burning tension that makes it feel like the veins are bursting out of my skin. Then I relax, and sweet emotions fill my heart like helium, and it feels like I'm about to glide up into the air any moment now. My eyes fill with tears, and I kiss my pillow with pure affection.

Gently, I disappear from this world into another world, where millennia go by in a second and a single moment takes an age to pass. I look around me with astonishment, like a visitor from outer space, watching how life rises and falls, how the ocean deepens and how the sky rises, how stars twinkle, and how new growth springs from the earth. Then I realize that it is me creating this world; it springs up from my footprints, which lie like a crooked path behind me as far as the eye can see. I'm both the creator and the created; I'm both the matter and the spirit, a fish in the sky and a bird in the ocean.

Chapter 34

Mom is sleepy in the bright morning light and yawns heavily. She asks me about the costume ball and laughs when I tell her about Peter in the chicken costume. She asks if I danced, but I quickly fill my mouth with cereal.

"A little," I say.

Trudy comes into the kitchen and says good morning in a happy voice. And now it's Mom's turn to answer some questions. Trudy asks her if she had fun and how it was, and I can tell by Mom's reaction that she doesn't want go into any details, any more than I do. She hands me my lunch box and reminds me that this is the last day of school before Easter, which makes my heart skip a beat in the bright morning.

At school I have a hard time pretending that Clara doesn't exist because if I turn in my seat, her tranquil eyes are fixed upon me.

The buds on the trees in the school yard are blossoming, the trees bobbing gently in the warm breeze. Peter stands by my side at morning break, talking about the inquest into the accident on the *Orca*.

"Does your dad get risk bonus?" he asks.

"He's not on that ship anymore," I say.

"Oh," he says, and it seems he's a little disappointed on my behalf. "What is he doing, then?"

"He has a fishing boat in the country, up on the lake, you know," I say.

"Really?" Peter says, and I can tell he thinks this is not nearly as exciting as having a father on a ship traveling all over the world.

"He's having a baby soon."

"He is?" Peter says joyfully. "And you're becoming a big brother," he says, and punches me on the shoulder. "I could teach you a lesson or two," he says. "Changing diapers and stuff." He laughs.

Then he becomes thoughtful for a moment.

"Is your dad moving here, then?" he asks suddenly, and I'm sure he's looking forward to visiting with me and teaching me how to handle babies.

"No, they're going to stay in the country," I say.

"I see," he says, and I feel his enthusiasm fade out.

Headmaster Pinko walks briskly into the classroom, and the math lesson begins. As usual he talks and talks and stands by the blackboard and writes up the example with white chalk or sits on the corner of the desk, loving the sound of his own voice going on and on. He goes over the homework examples one by one, explaining each thoroughly and talking and talking because life is math and math is life. I'm horrified to realize that I have done everything wrong. Not one example in my notebook is right, and I'm miles off even in the most simple ones. I just don't have a math brain. It's as simple as that. It's all right to make one mistake in an example or two — Pinko just finds that endearing and amusing, because it also gives him a chance to let his bright light of wisdom shine forth. But to have every one completely wrong is nothing less than stupidity in his eyes.

When he's gone over all the examples and has explained it all over and over, he wipes the blackboard completely clean, and a knot of anxiety explodes in my stomach. He writes a new example on the board, turns, smiling, faces the class, rubs his hands together, and adjusts his specs on his nose. He's going to take someone up.

"Now, this is a real challenge," he says, and winks at the class while the poor kid who has been picked out stands there racking his brain to the sound of the class giggling. Pinko smirks and whistles a little tune and looks at the boy, who can barely hold the chalk with his trembling fingers.

"No, no," Pinko says, laughing, when the boy thinks he's finished. "You don't put x^2 there!" Pinko says. "Not there! Ha, ha!"

And the class laughs with him, but the eyes of the victim search wildly in vain for the place to put x^2.

Pinko's bald head glistens, and his white shirt stands out, luminous, against his red tie, his gray suit impeccable, the crease on his trousers sharp as a razor blade. Confidently and helpfully, he leads the boy out of the maze and then sends him, shaking, back to his seat, where he quickly wipes the sweat off his head with his sleeve.

Pinko writes another example on the blackboard and turns around, smiling.

"Well," he says brightly. "Who wants to come up here and show us how to solve this?"

At once everybody tries to lie low except for the math geeks, who raise their hands eagerly, even though they know as well as us, the normal geeks, that they won't be chosen. He looks from one face to the next, and I'm starting to suspect who this game is meant for. Somewhere in this class is a boy who lets his imagination get the better of him.

His eyes fall to rest on me.

"Josh Stephenson. Come here and show us how it's done," he says with false pleasantness.

The silence is buzzing in my ears.

I stand up slowly. The legs of the chair screech over the floor. I step out of the row, resting my hand on the desk, then put one leg carefully in front of the other. There's a low creak of the floorboards every time I put my foot down. It's the only sound I can hear.

Ahead of me is the teacher's desk. Pinko stands smiling with the white chalk in his hand. As I get closer I can see the white dust on his fingers and an almost invisible cloud of dust on his gray jacket sleeve. I'm up at the desk, and all eyes are fixed on the back of my head. I stop by the blackboard, and Pinko's thick fingers hand me the chalk. I raise my hand slowly and take it without looking up.

"Well. What's the solution?" he says.

I can almost hear the corners of his mouth rise and his lips stretch over his teeth as he smiles over the classroom.

There's nothing I would like to do more than solve this. Solve it with such a stroke of genius that nothing like it has ever been seen. Solve it completely. Absolutely. Just to show him that I can, just to get my revenge on him. But I know I can't. And he knows it too.

"C'mon, now. We're waiting," he says, smiling, and his bald head gleams and the swollen artery on his neck beats the rhythm, tight against the snow-white collar of his shirt. He's like the shark, *Carcharodon carcharias,* who nibbles on his prey until it stops fighting, killing it slowly just for fun with sharp yellow teeth, all of them pointing into its mouth. When the prey is past the first row of teeth, there's no hope of escape; it can flee in only one direction: farther down the bloody jaw. So perfect a killing machine is the shark, so merciless and selfish.

"The bee," I say in a quiet, trembling voice.

"Talk louder, Josh, so everyone can hear you."

"The bee," I say louder.

"Huh? This isn't natural history, my boy. That was yesterday, ha, ha, ha!"

A nervous laughter gushes out of the class for a moment, but then everything falls silent.

"Carry on," he orders but his smile has gone.

"The bee is one of the greatest wonders of nature," I say.

He knocks softly on the blackboard, and the white clouds of chalk dust twirl from under his fist.

"The example on the blackboard, Josh."

But now all I can see are the pages of *Life and Creation*, where I wrote down everything the narrator said about the bee, *Apis mellifera*.

I raise my voice, and the words burst out of me.

"The bee is one of the greatest wonders of nature and the bee community is one of the most advanced in the whole animal kingdom!"

I fill my lungs with air, and I can't even hear what Pinko is saying.

"After impregnation takes place in the air, the male bee dies, but the queen bee preserves millions of eggs, which she lays gradually over the course of her lifetime!"

The shark grabs my shoulder, shaking me harshly, but I'm not going to let him stop me. I tear myself free and grab a tight hold on the teacher's desk, and the words come screaming out of my mouth.

"The first bees to hatch are the worker bees, then service bees, who take care of the queen and bring her food day and night, and the worker bees go out in the field to gather nectar from thousands of flowers, which they change into honey!" I scream, my face boiling with anger.

"Shut up! Go back to your seat!" Pinko just barely manages to shout. He grabs my arm to loosen my grip on the desk, but then I grab his jacket tightly and hang there and scream straight into his face.

"The bee has tens of thousands of eyes and fourteen thousand delicate sensors that sense the environment, but these are the most important sense organs because with their eyes, they map the position of certain flowers, and their sensors are indispensable in communicating with other bees in the colony, but the communications of bees are much more complicated than we thought they were!" I scream at the top of my lungs, hanging on to Pinko's jacket.

He's trying to drag me to the door and is reaching for the doorknob. The whole class is standing now, staring in paralyzed horror.

"In the bee community, individuals work together and help one another and no one is left out, because every bee has a unique position and is indispensable to the whole!"

Pinko opens the door, rips me off him, throws me out of the classroom, and slams the door. I jump to my feet and try to open the door, but he pushes against me until I hear the key turn as he locks the door. Then I scream the last sentences into the keyhole.

"And we humans could learn a lot from the bees if we would admit that everybody is equally important and that everyone has their value and that without them, the work of the others would come to nothing!"

I hear the class laughing and whistling on the other side of the door. A few are clapping their hands, chairs and desks screech on the floor, and the teacher's stick smacks loudly when Pinko hits the desk with it, howling, "Silence! Silence!"

I sit in the school yard, waiting for the bell to chime so I can go in and get my schoolbag. I couldn't care less if anybody laughs at me or if Pinko punishes me; it doesn't matter. I'm not afraid of anything. The bee is, and always will be, a greater miracle than all the math in the world. And if you understand the bee, it doesn't matter what you know about math. What's the mathematical formula for honey? Nobody knows that. Except the bee.

The bell rings loudly, and immediately the screeching sound from desks and chairs carries out of the open windows across the playground. Then the trembling drum solo begins as each class runs down the steps and the children jump out the door and run like darts over the playground, out of the gate. Some take it easy and start kicking a ball around. Someone is talking about going on a ski trip. Another about all the Easter eggs that are waiting for him. The third sings the national anthem.

I move behind the trees so I can't be seen from the front door when my class comes running out.

"He's crazy!" I hear someone shout.

"No, it was great!" another one says.

"He's mental. Where did he go?"

I peek around the tree truck and see Peter standing by the steps, holding my schoolbag, looking around. But I sit tight because I don't want to talk to him right now. I listen to the crunching gravel when he, the last of the crowd, leaves the playground. When he has disappeared out the gate, I stand up and start walking toward the gate.

"There you are," her voice says. I turn, and she's standing before me in her red coat with the silk scarf around her neck and pearl drops in each ear. She's holding my bag in her hand.

"There you go," she says, and hands it to me.

"Thanks," I say as I take it.

She has white mittens on and there are blue frost roses knitted on the backs of the hands.

"That was one great speech," she says, smiling.

I'm a little awkward and don't know what to say, but try to smile and look for a while up in the clouds and then I look sternly over the playground like I'm searching for something specific to rest my eyes on.

"He was so mad, the old geezer," she says with a laugh.

"Yeah?" I say, and run my fingers through my hair.

"Shall we walk?" she says.

"Yeah, sure," I say, and we walk across the playground and out the gate.

We don't talk for a long while, but the sound of our steps on the sidewalk is almost in rhythm.

"Did you just make all that up, or do you know all about it?" she asks.

Out of the corner of my eye, I see her put her hair behind her ear so the pearl drop is more visible.

I hear myself start to speak and tell her about my

notebook, *Life and Creation,* and that I've written down everything I've ever learned about natural history and zoology. And my mouth goes on talking, telling her that I think we can learn so much by researching animals and nature, because life isn't just math, like Pinko says, but something quite different and far more magnificent. And my mouth continues on and on, and she listens intently and asks questions and my voice answers her. And her voice starts to tell me about some things that she's been thinking about along those lines. And my ears listen. My voice agrees with her, and we talk like that and listen alternately. Our voices are braided together in front of us and around us and weave around each other, like long colored bands of silk. They untangle and tangle again, like fingers searching for each other so they can hold hands.

Suddenly we're standing in front of her house. She takes her keys out of her red coat pocket. On the key ring hangs one of the seven dwarfs, holding a lantern.

"Would you like to come in?" she asks.

"Sure," I say.

The hall is about the size of my bedroom, the living room as big as our whole apartment. There are three big windows with cream-colored blinds with lace trimmings and heavy dark-green curtains on each side trimmed with golden cord.

"Go in," she says, and I walk slowly into the living room, past two vases, about the size of a six-year-old child. By a light-brown leather sofa stands a coffee table with gold feet and a smoky glass top. Beyond that are two leather chairs, matching the sofa, square with low backs and arms and soft corners. A painting on the wall shows a glorious mountain view, and another, large fields overgrown with birch in the glimmering sunlight. On another wall are several items from distant corners of the world: an African mask, an Arabic knife, a Chinese drawing.

"Have a seat," she says, and points to the sofa.

The pleasant-smelling leather creaks softly as I sit down. I stare at the bookcases, which reach up to the ceiling. The luminous gold lettering on the red and brown leather spines glints under the lights inside the cases.

By another wall is a huge cupboard with sandblasted glass containing a single row of porcelain teacups on a glass shelf. The dining-room table is shiny with six chairs around it. In the middle of the table is a finely knitted cloth, and on it stands a blue glass vase with fresh-cut flowers.

"Would you like something to drink?" she asks, but disappears into the kitchen without waiting for an answer.

I feel strange and dig my toes into the thick carpet and feel it move and squash under the weight of my feet. It's like time stands still in here, like nothing will ever change. There's enough time for everything, like sitting for a long while in a soft leather chair, reading a good book. Enough time to sit at the table, chatting with guests. In this great house, the whole family can live their independent lives in spacious bedrooms and large living rooms, enjoying their family rituals and deep family traditions forever.

She appears in the door between the two vases, with lemonade in two tall glasses that must be for special occasions, and fetches two pearl-knitted coasters from a special box on the glass table. She probably made these coasters herself in Sewing Club at school. It's like they have been made for the single purpose of being placed on this table. She places one mat in front of me and hands me the glass.

"There you are."

"Thank you," I say, and take hold of the ice-cold glass.

She lights two lamps, and the warm light glitters off every object. It's also like no dust ever falls on anything in here, and that's why nobody ever has to vacuum or wipe or polish or scrub the floors. Everything here is perfect and constant. There are no worries or troubles, only harmony and tranquillity.

"Did you have fun at the dance?" she asks as she puts her glass on the mat and pulls her feet in close to her onto the chair. She's wearing a short black skirt and black tights.

"It was all right," I say. "You just disappeared?" I add.

"I was hoping you'd come out to walk me home," she says.

"I didn't see you."

"I waited anyway. I really wanted to talk with you."

"Really?" I say, and tighten my grip around the thick bottom of the glass.

"Yes," she says.

"Oh," I say, and try to find a spot for my eyes to rest on.

She looks at her glass on the smoky tabletop and slowly puts her hair behind her right ear so the pearl drop glitters.

"I wanted to thank you for your poems," she says, and I feel the heat rise and fall in my face. "It was you who put them in my bag, right?"

"Yes," I whisper into my glass.

"They're really beautiful," she says.

I look away, red in the face, not knowing what to say next. Then I see the dark-green curtains that weren't supposed to touch the floor of our living room while Mom was sewing them. So here they hang, obviously never used to cover the windows; they are just for decoration. All those nights she slaved and stayed up late to finish them on time. For decoration. I can't remember a single poem, as if I never really wrote any of them. But I did write them to her, whom I loved more than anything in this life. And there she is sitting opposite me, a little shy, like me, waiting for me to say something, to explain why I wrote these poems and put them in her schoolbag. But I can't say anything because I have nothing to say. I don't know anymore if the one I love is real or not. Maybe she exists only in my little notebook; maybe that's her real home.

"I'm thinking about taking some dance classes after Easter," she says. "There's a spring course in ballroom dancing."

"Really?" I say, relieved that she broke the silence.

"Yes," she says. "I love to dance, you know."

"I see," I say, even more embarrassed, remembering my clumsy steps at the costume ball.

"I was thinking, you see, because I really need a partner, if you were maybe interested in coming with me."

"Me?"

"Yes."

"I don't know."

"You know, it's not the kind of dances you dance at school dances; these are real dances, waltzes and things like that. It's maybe twice a week. Then we would have to practice, of course, on our own. Don't you think it would be fun? We could easily practice here in my basement. There's lots of room. And Mom and Dad have tons of CDs with the right kind of music."

She goes on talking and explaining waltzes to me and quickstep and rumba, and I can't put a word in because she is so eager and happy to be able to talk about something so we aren't just sitting in awkward silence.

How lovely and sweet she is to me, just because I fell in love with her and wrote her poems. How utterly caring she is not to make jokes about it, or tell anyone, but instead invite me into her home and give me lemonade. And as a poet's reward, she invites me to dance with her. In a spring class, in ballroom dancing, where we would learn quickstep and rumba and then practice in her basement all summer.

Sometimes it happens, every million years or so, that two stars come so close to each other that they almost touch. But just barely. And only every million years or so.

"The thing is," I say, after a short silence, "that I'm moving away."

"Away?" she says, surprised, her eyes growing wider.

"Yes," I say. "To my father's."

"Where is that?"

"In the country."

"So far?"

"Yes."

Again there's silence in the living room, long enough for me to hear the ticking of a grandfather clock, which I hadn't noticed before. It stands by the wall, behind the dining-room table, and beside it hangs a small painting, a portrait of an old lady with a colorful shawl over her shoulders. The low ticking of the clock is both soft and resilient, and I can just imagine that when the clock strikes, the sound is somehow in harmony with everything in here; a refined sound, made by a small silver hammer on copper springs. And I realize suddenly that time doesn't stand still in this house any longer.

"When do you leave?"

"Soon."

"You're going for good, then?"

"I don't know. Most likely."

"I see," she says in a low voice. "It's a bit of a surprise."

"Yes," I say.

Then we're silent for a while, sipping our lemonade. The ticking clock becomes uncomfortably loud in my ears.

"Well," I say, "I really have to go now."

I stand up from the chair, and the creaking leather follows my movement. When I've stood up, the leather continues to creak softly, moving back into shape, like the skin on the palm of a hand, opening slowly.

She follows me across the carpet, into the tile-decorated hall. While I put my shoes on, she stands before me with her arms crossed over her chest and has put her hair behind both ears. Suddenly her eyes are so wide and her face doesn't radiate the charming smile it did. When I've put my coat on, she looks so small and thin with her arms crossed like that, tight to her red sweater, the collar of her white shirt lying over the collar of her sweater. I try not to look straight at her but just a little past her, because her eyes are looking at me searchingly and I know my face is red.

"Thank you," I say, and nod, and then have just about enough courage to look her in the eye for a brief second. But then something passes quickly over her eyes; the wishing stones are glittering in the deep clear water. She places her arms around my neck, embraces my head, and places her warm cheek next to mine.

"Oh, Josh," she whispers.

She holds me tight, and her heart is beating hard into my thick coat. I look over her shoulder at my hand, gently stroking her back, her long black hair. I rest it there for a while. The grandfather clock strikes the hour, and the sound is exactly as I imagined it. I close my eyes, feeling her hair under the palm of my hand, her hands wrapped around my head, our bodies tight together, her breath caressing my cheek.

Isn't it strange how the sweetest dreams are just about to come true, the moment you realize they're just that—sweet dreams—and you can't wait to wake up to the reality of your true self?

Chapter 35

The church is full to the brim, and the air vibrates from the thundering organ and the voices from the choir. Trudy and I move our lips with a hymn book in our hands, but Mom sings loudly by my side. All of those who endured the long winter in the half-empty church, while God slept, sit here now. But all the others praise him only on this day, just in case. There's no loose floorboard by my feet where we sit now, but that doesn't matter because I don't need to wake God up today. If my mom's singing doesn't keep him awake and make the resurrection happen, I can't imagine what else could bring Jesus back to life.

> *"Hear the joyful news from throne up high*
> *That hope will bring our world, so poor and sad.*
> *See angels of the Lord give out a cry:*
> *Our brother, Christ, is risen from the dead."*

Dad called the other day to talk to her. I was lying on the living-room floor, pretending to watch a movie, but all my attention was focused on the hallway, where Mom was sitting with the phone in her hand. For a long time, she said nothing but just listened to what he was saying. When she finally spoke, her voice was so low that I couldn't hear a thing. After their conversation was over, she sat by the phone for a while, distant and distracted, but then she went into the kitchen, and a moment later, I could smell cigarette smoke. When the movie was over and I had finished the chocolate cookies and my drink, she came into the living room with a cup of coffee and sat in her chair. Then I could tell that the time had come. Right there in the stillness of the evening before we would say good night to each other.

"Do you want to go to your dad's?" she asked.

"Yes," I said, but immediately felt I didn't want to have to say this. But I had to say it anyway. It was what I wanted.

"Well, dear. So you've been thinking things over?" she said.

"Yes," I replied, picking up loose threads from the gray carpet, rolling them into a ball between my fingertips.

"That's good. I think it will do you both good. Boys need their fathers as well, you know." Then she was silent for a moment, before continuing, making it sound as if these were quite practical and appropriate measures.

"He's going to help you with math, he told me. I think your headmaster will agree to letting you take the summer exams in the country, if it can be arranged. It will all turn out fine, I'm sure of it."

But when she said this it was like something had broken inside me. Not with any noise, but silently. Blinking, I crawled up on my knees and hid my head in her lap.

"I also want to stay here with you," I whispered.

"Of course you do," she said, stroking my hair. "But sometimes we have to choose. That's life."

She took my head in both her hands and looked at me for a long time: her eyes blue, with thin white patterns in the blue; around her pupils a dark blue circle, which made the white even whiter, the blue even bluer. Her face in the half-light was so young and fresh, her hair wavy and her forehead smooth. Her eyebrows delicate and her nose straight. When she smiled, the corners of her mouth made dimples form in her cheeks and her eyes brighten.

"But you must promise me," she said, "never to shirk your duties. Sometimes we feel life is not fair, but then we shouldn't run away, but face our problems and hope for the best. That's how you become a grown-up," she said, and her eyes sparkled like she was looking into my soul.

The thundering organ fills the church with a blasting sound again, and the singers raise their powerful voices. At once, the bright sound of a trumpet soars, weaving itself in with the majestic harmony, and everybody stands up. It is a bit hard not to join in the singing because I can feel my soul expand inside me. And why shouldn't I sing properly if I feel like it? So I raise my voice with the choir, in the safe shelter of my mom's singing.

Christ is in his place on the altar painting, floating in midair between heaven and earth. Above him is the eternal light of the heavens, but below him Roman soldiers are rolling in the dirt. It looks like any moment now, Jesus will glide up and out of the painting. His face is handsome and bright, and his long hair falls in soft waves over his naked shoulders. He is probably quite relieved to be free from the tomb. Maybe he was worried that the angels weren't going to be able to lift the stone. He is on his way to his father, and I know he must be looking forward to meeting him, just as I am. And even though, as it says in the Bible, it was two thousand years ago that he went up to heaven, I still wish him a safe journey in my mind, just in case.

When we're home, Mom makes herself some coffee and starts to prepare the Easter dinner. Trudy and I, however, finish moving her furniture into my room. My books are now in boxes, which I have stacked up against the wall in the small room that used to be her room. It will be my storage room now. The things from my desk filled up a whole box: drawings, notebooks, paint, pencils, brushes, and a small jar with shiny coins from the beach. I took the postcards from Dad off the wall and put them in the shoe box, then placed it in the box and closed it. On top of that one, I stacked two boxes filled with books.

We carry my bed, my chair, and my desk into the storage room. Trudy will keep my bookcase for her books. Finally there's nothing in the room to suggest that I was ever here, except for the fish tank on the chest of drawers in the corner. The sound of the water pump is different now that Trudy's furniture is in here.

Mom puts the lamb in the oven and adjusts the timer on the stove while Trudy takes a bath and puts on her favorite dress. I fetch the plates, glasses, and silverware and place it all on the dining table in the living room. When the doorbell rings, I go to the door. There stands Auntie Carol, in her best Sunday dress, with rollers in her hair under her scarf. She always asks Mom to do her hair for holidays and celebrations. She has a huge plate in her hands.

"There," she says, handing me the plate. "I'm not buying chocolate eggs for half-grown men."

Under the shiny plastic cover is the one and only pear tart, just because I'm leaving. She really can be so kind.

She hangs up her coat and sits in the kitchen and starts to take the rollers out of her hair. Then the chatting and familiar kitchen noises begin. Carol struggles to watch quietly when things are being done differently from how she would do them. She insists the potatoes should be caramelized. Mom asks her to make the sauce instead, because she does it so much better then Mom ever could. And they joke with each other, with aprons over their pretty dresses, and Mom hurries to do Carol's hair so she can start making the sauce. Trudy sits at the kitchen table, her face made up, earrings dangling down to her naked shoulders. She is opening cans of green peas and carrots. She is anxious and excited today, and I know why. Her new boyfriend has asked her to the movies tomorrow night. He doesn't have a motorcycle but a real monster of a car with fat tires and spoilers and all. It's probably much more enjoyable riding in that kind of vehicle than hanging on to the back of a motorcycle in all kinds of weather.

The lamb is on the table. There are glistening caramelized potatoes in a bowl, steam rising from the red cabbage, green peas, carrots, and sweet-smelling sauce. Grandma's silver spoon stands upright in dark-red cranberry sauce in a small crystal bowl. Mom pours my favorite soda mix in the high glasses with the sandblasted flower pattern. Auntie Carol, with her hair beautifully done, carves the lamb, since she is so clever with the knife, as Mom puts it.

When Trudy and I are finishing clearing the table, and Mom and Auntie Carol are in the kitchen washing up, the doorbell rings. There stands Peter in the dim light; it's almost dark. He places two fingers at his brow and flicks them away casually. "Sir."

I repeat the gesture, and we laugh as we go inside.

"Come on in," I say. "There's a huge slice of pear tart in here with your name on it."

On the dining-room table is the mouthwatering pear tart from Auntie Carol, the ultimate prize. I dig the knife into the soft icing and cut a big piece for Peter. We sit for a long while just gobbling up this unbelievable treat, our only conversation our happy sighs and murmurs of satisfaction.

With our stomachs full and smiles on our faces, we go up

to my room. Peter stops on the threshold because nothing is the way it used to be.

On the floor is my suitcase, ready to go.

"When are you leaving?"

"Dad's on his way now."

Peter sits on my cousin's bed. He looks a little confused, like he doesn't know what to say. Finally he stands up, walks over to the fish tank, and looks into the water for a long time, like he's searching for something.

"I guess we won't be publishing the magazine, then?" he asks.

"I guess not," I say.

"It was a really good idea, anyway," he says.

"Yes, it was. It was a great idea," I say.

I hear Trudy on the phone, talking to her boyfriend, Mom and Auntie Carol in the kitchen, the sounds of their voices trickling up the stairs. Then there's the sound of a car stopping outside and the engine still running. The horn honks twice. It's Dad.

"He's here," Mom calls.

Peter thrusts his hand in his pocket and takes out a small chocolate Easter egg, wrapped in red foil.

"Just for fun," he says, and hands it to me.

"Thanks," I say.

"Well, I guess you're going now," he says.

"Yes," I say.

"I should go too," he says.

I follow him to the front door. When he's on the doorstep, I tell him that I'll call him when I get to my father's and he nods.

And because I guess we won't be seeing each other for some time, I raise a stiff hand to my forehead, curve my eyebrows, make the harsh soldier face that Peter finds so funny, and puff my chest out.

"Dismissed! Farewell, Peter Johnson!"

He doesn't react immediately but hesitates for a moment. His lips move like he's searching for words. His face is all red, and when he puts his hand to his forehead, his hand isn't stiff and firm as it should be when you salute. He just rubs his eyebrow in an awkward manner with his fingers and shifts his weight from one foot to the other.

"Safe journey, Josh Stephenson," he says finally, and turns around abruptly, runs down the stairs, and disappears out the front door.

But then I suddenly remember what I had completely forgotten and rush upstairs, into my little storage room. Mom and Trudy call after me, telling me to bring down my suitcase, but there is no time to answer them because I have to catch Peter before he gets home.

I hurriedly put my shoes on in the hall as Mom and Dad stand, utterly astonished, outside the front door in the dull evening light.

"Where are you going with that?" Mom asks.

"I'll be quick," I say, and run down the street into the gathering darkness.

Under the streetlight, green sprouts are sticking their heads out of the earth in their gardens. Soon they'll turn into Easter lilies. There's nobody on the streets, but lights are lit in every window. In the warm light, families are sitting at their dining tables. All these different people, in all these different houses, all doing the same thing.

I run down the alleyway because I have to catch Peter before he gets home. I call his name, and in the twilight I think I see his silhouette hesitating, as if he expected me. I run harder, and a sudden gust of wind catches the wings of Christian the Ninth in my arms; they flutter as if he has come alive. The light gleams in his eager eyes, as if he's more than ready to help my very good friend on his journey to freedom, the journey we all must take, everyone in our own way.

A Note on the Translation

Fish in the Sky was originally written in Icelandic, the author's mother tongue, and was translated into English by the author himself for publication. Halfway through the editing process, a translation by Bernard Scudder was brought to light. This translation was immensely helpful during this process.

Sadly, Bernard Scudder died in his prime shortly after his manuscript was found. He had lived in Iceland for decades. His obituary in the *Guardian* described him as "a poet and the doyen of translators of Icelandic literature into English."

His deep understanding and love for the Icelandic language shows through in all his work, from translations of the sagas to contemporary poetry and literature.